T0161356

Also by
Michael Farris Smith

Nick
Blackwood
The Fighter
Desperation Road
Rivers

THE
HANDS OF
STRANGERS

MICHAEL FARRIS SMITH

BLAIR

Durham, NC

© 2011 by Michael Farris Smith
Cover Design by Laura Williams
Typeset in Fairfield by Copperline Book Services.

This book is a work of fiction. As in all fiction, the literary perceptions
and insights are based on experience; however, all names, characters, places,
and incidents are either products of the author's imagination or are used
fictitiously. No reference to any real person is intended or should be
inferred.

The first chapter of *The Hands of Strangers* first appeared in slightly
different form as a story titled "Anywhere" in *The Summerset Review.*

Previously published in 2011 by Main Street Rag Publishing
and in first ebook edition in 2014 by Simon & Schuster.

Library of Congress Cataloging-in-Publication Data
Names: Smith, Michael F. (Michael Farris), 1970– author.
Title: The hands of strangers / Michael Farris Smith.
Description: Durham, NC : Carolina Wren Press, [2017]
Identifiers: LCCN 2016058604 |
ISBN 9780932112712 (softcover : acid-free paper)
Subjects: LCSH: Missing children—Fiction. | Paris (France)—
Fiction. | Domestic fiction.
Classification: LCC PS3619.M592234 H36 2017 | DDC 813/.6 —dc23
LC record available at https://lccn.loc.gov/2016058604

For Sabrea

Le rayon d'en haut does not always shine upon us and may well be hidden behind clouds, but without that light a man cannot live and is worth nothing and can do no good, and those who claim that man can live without faith in that higher light and need not trouble to acquire it, are sure to have their hopes dashed.

—VINCENT VAN GOGH IN A LETTER TO HIS BROTHER, THEO VAN GOGH

1

When it comes you will know it, when it comes you will know it, Jon repeated to himself. It came and went and he didn't know it until two stops past. He had counted before he got on the metro. Eight stops. And he counted because he wasn't able to see the signs on the wall in the metro halls, the bodies crammed together, a mob of Parisian heads surrounding him and crowding the door in the evening's busiest hour. So he counted and stood in the middle and subtracted one at each stop. He had three to go and that's when he began repeating When it comes you will know it. And then he started thinking about Estelle at home in the apartment, sitting next to the telephone, organizing their flyer campaign for high-traffic street corners and bus stops and metro lines, and now he realizes he's two stops past.

"Goddammit," he mumbles, and a man holding a bag of groceries looks at him blankly.

The plan was for Jon to be in prime position to hand out the flyers in the Gare du Nord metro station before the six o'clock crowd, but he stopped for a drink that became three. He knows Estelle won't know. She won't leave that phone in case the police call and she trusts him to do this right but he had to have a drink. He can't help but have a drink before he goes into the metro with a stack of orange flyers that have a picture of his nine-year-old daughter in the middle, surrounded with AIDEZ-NOUS À RETROUVER JENNIFER written in bold black letters. He simply can't help it.

The metro stops and he bumps out of the door with a pack of others. He moves with the crowd along the passageways of the rue Montmartre stop. It takes going up and down stairs and through a rounded hallway to get to the other side of the tracks. People are everywhere and in a steady shuffle, ready to get home, put up their feet, have their dinner, read their paper. The train arrives and this time he concentrates, gets on late so he can stand near the door, see out of the window. Back two stops to Gare du Nord, where five metro lines and half of Paris collide and there is every kind of face—old, pretty, tired, laughing, cynical, white, brown, round, thin, childish, hollow. No matches for Jennifer. No little girl with thin, wavy hair and green eyes, wearing jeans and a pink backpack and her heavy coat. Two months and nothing. Two months of her dancing in his head in this outfit. He stops at the foot of the escalator, where people cluster in an impatient pack, and passes out the orange flyers. Some take, some ignore. The ones that take fold and stuff it without looking, maybe will find it later when they reach into their pockets or purses as they pay for bread on the walk home, will say to themselves, *Where did this come from?* And he wonders the same. This day, this moment, this getting here, this standing at the escalator. Where did this come from? This slow, slow ticking of the clock. The crowd thins as the time between trains expands, and out of a stack of two hundred flyers, he keeps five to post on the exits that lead up into the streets.

He gets onto the escalator and the woman on the step in front of him sees what he's holding and says, "I have seen this. On the news. You haven't found her yet?"

Jon shakes his head and says, "Not yet."

"You should go on television again," she says and turns away. He feels confident that if universal law allowed it, he could put his hands around her neck and choke her until her mouth was dry.

The walkways' and intersections' exits and entrances are organized chaos and he is nearly knocked down over and over working his way through the traffic. When he's done sticking up the last one, he looks at his watch and times for thirty seconds, then counts how many people look at their flyer.

Two. Which is up one from last week when he posted at the Gare de l'Est.

He gets on the metro and heads back home. At the café at the end of his street Monsieur Conrer serves him another drink, and when he goes into the apartment Estelle is perched on a stool next to the phone in the kitchen, cigarette in one hand and red marker in the other. She looks up, smokes, then says, "How'd it go?"

◥

They have stopped sleeping in the same room because they don't sleep. Estelle takes the couch and Jon lies in the bedroom. He hears her all hours of the night—pacing, opening the refrigerator door, changing channels. Jon tries to trick himself into sleeping by imagining they're on a long vacation and Jennifer is left behind with friends. Sometimes Estelle will come into the bedroom and crawl over close to him, rest her head on his chest, curl herself into a ball. She is a combination of smells—of perfume, of cigarettes, of coffee. But she doesn't ever stay curled next to him for long.

On empty afternoons, when alone in the apartment, each of them has tried to go into Jennifer's room and make her bed, put her shoes away in the closet, close the teen fashion magazine lying open on her nightstand. Jon had laughed when she held it out to him in the bookstore and said she needed it. "Need? Nine is a single-digit number. That information is for girls with double-digit birthdays." She looked down at it, ran her hand across the glossy cover, as if she could feel herself in the perfect face staring back at her. "Let's just pretend I'm twelve," she said. He took it and made her promise not to tell her mother. Which she did the moment they walked into the apartment. Later that night, with Jennifer asleep between them on the couch, Estelle had reached over and playfully smacked the back of Jon's head and said, "Don't rush her."

So they go into the room, but tiptoe around the way it is. Careful not to disrupt her life. They keep the door half open, giving themselves a glimpse of the life that was as they walk down the hallway.

Even life upside down has its routine. Estelle stays at home on high alert but Jon has to go to work because the earth keeps spinning. So he shows up at L'École des Langues at nine a.m. every weekday morning, goes to his desk, assorts his tasks for the day, and then the knocks and bumps of an office distract him until he walks back into the street in the evening. His coworkers can't figure out how to treat him. Too normal and they risk apathy. Too sympathetic and they become patronizing. What he gets are overly cautious smiles when he's handed a fax or offered a smoke or asked about something he should have done already. Hidden sympathy in tiny gestures that he appreciates but he would rather them kick a hole in the side of his desk and scream, "What the fuck is the world coming to!"

This is the story they were told—Jennifer's class went to the Musée d'Orsay with their teacher and a volunteer parent. A typical field trip in a typical Paris day. She was there as they sat in a circle in front of a van Gogh. She was there as they sat in a circle in front of a Cézanne. She was there when they ate their sack lunches in the courtyard. She was not there when they counted heads to walk to the bus stop to go back to school. She was not there as the teacher retraced their footsteps. She was not in the bathroom. She was not in the gift shop. She was not in the snack area buying a chocolate bar, which she had a tendency to do on field trips. She was not anywhere.

Their flyer campaign is in full swing and twice a week after work Jon goes through the same routine he went through at the Gare du Nord. They change colors from orange to yellow. Estelle thinks they are easier to read in passing. They try a larger-size paper. They move the telephone numbers of the apartment and of the detective from the bottom to the top.

After doing his duty at the Place d'Italie metro station, Jon stops at Monsieur Conrer's café next door to their apartment building. It's winter and dark at 6:30, the lights from the shops glowing yellow in the early night. He knows Estelle is waiting but he can't go up, not yet ready to hide his despair. Monsieur Conrer has a glass of whiskey waiting for him as he comes in.

"Where today?" he says as Jon sits down at the bar.

"Place d'Italie."

"A good spot. Something will happen," he says. His hair is thin and silver and his shoulders slump. He has his own children and grandchildren and he has cried for Jennifer. It happened a week after she disappeared. Jon talked Estelle out of the apartment on a Saturday afternoon and they came and sat here at the table by the window. They shared a carafe of wine and Jon got up to go to the bathroom. When he came back, M. Conrer was sitting with Estelle, they held hands across the table, and they both cried quietly. Jon stepped back into the bathroom and watched through the cracked door until they were finished. Ever since, this is one of the few places she will go. M. Conrer tells Jon every day, "You are one day closer to having Jennifer home." Jon drinks the first whiskey and asks for another.

"Estelle came in for lunch today," M. Conrer says.

Jon hears him but doesn't answer. M. Conrer lays his pack of cigarettes in front of Jon and he takes one.

This time, when the old man tells him you're one day closer, Jon says, "The chances are dying by the minute. I've read the books."

"Don't think like that."

"That's the least of what I think. If you could see what I think, you'd throw up on your shoes."

"Don't think that either," he says.

But Jon has. And does. Is there only one? Or two or four, or do they rotate, charge a fee, bring them down a thin alley, into a short door, sell her off in ten-minute intervals. Are there women too? He doesn't want to think these thoughts and he fights them when they arrive but they are as real as his hands and feet. When he prays, he prays that she can at least be given a civil abduction. M. Conrer reaches over with the bottle and makes it a double. Then the bell on the door jingles and

Estelle walks in and takes a stool beside Jon.

"Detective Marceau called and said he has seen the flyers and that we're doing a good job," she says and this has given her a satisfaction, a hope that he notices in her eyebrows.

"Good. Did he say anything else?"

"Only that they're working hard. And that maybe we should up the reward." She takes a cigarette from M. Conrer's pack. "Was Place d'Italie a very busy spot?"

No, it wasn't.

"Yeah, pretty busy," he answers.

"Can we go up to thirty thousand?"

They started at fifteen. After a month they went to twenty. "Whatever we need to do," Jon says and makes the mistake of sighing.

"That didn't sound very convincing."

"I said whatever we need to do."

"It's the *way* you said it."

"Estelle. A million. I don't care. I'm on your side."

"Don't talk to me like that," she says and throws her cigarette at him. "Maybe we should just quit. Just quit and move away and act like we never had a daughter."

"Gimme a goddamn break. I'm tired."

"And I'm not?" she says and bangs her fist on the bar. Then she's up and crying before she can get out of the door.

He knocks off the drink and asks for another.

"Are you sure you want another?" M. Conrer says.

"I don't know." He shakes his head, then points at the empty glass. "Yeah, I'm sure," he says. "Just let me sit." M. Conrer pours and walks away, gives him the solitude he asks for. Jon watches as the old man moves to other customers, offers matches, chats about the weather, and wonders if he would be so certain, so comforting, if one of his children were forever nine years old.

M. Conrer finally says he's not pouring any more. Jon leaves without paying and takes the metro to Saint-Michel. He thought whiskey warmed but the wind blows through his light jacket and he shivers as he moves up rue Saint-Séverin through the neon and smell of lamb. He makes his way through the Latin Quarter and to the river and walks along the sidewalk.

Nighttime dinner cruises ease by, waiters in tuxedos delivering wine and salads to the tables of the brightly lit cabins. A white foam trailing the boats. A misty rain starting to fall. He reaches the Pont des Arts and the lights of Paris—the high-priced apartments lining the river, the illumination of Notre-Dame behind him, the way the spotlights of the Louvre reach into the clouds—even in the damp night they are golden, something heavenly. He had stood there with Jennifer many times, and once, as she looked down into the river and what surrounded them, she said, "If I jumped I bet I could fly." Then she thought about it and said, "Or probably drown." He figured she was too light to drown, but fly, maybe. And he said, "I feel certain you'd fly but let's not try it today." She held out her arms and swayed. "Like this," she said. "I'd fly like this."

He turns up the collar on his coat and walks toward the Musée d'Orsay.

It's several blocks, time enough for the mist to wet his face and dampen his hair. He and Estelle walked this neighborhood for days, in all directions from the museum, looking for Jennifer's backpack or barrette or ID card. She's a smart little girl, he kept assuring Estelle, smart enough to leave a sign. But after days, then weeks, he'd admitted to himself that they weren't smart enough to find it. On the sidewalk along the river, a bench faces the front doors of the museum and he believes if he sits there long enough, Jennifer will come around the corner, or stick her head from around a tree and say, "Ha! Remember that time you grounded me for stealing your cigars and selling them on the playground? Got you back!"

He moves along through the mist, and when he gets to the bench, it's already occupied. With Estelle.

"Can I sit down?" he asks.

She looks up and says, "The way you wobbled along the sidewalk, you'd probably better."

She's more prepared for the night than he, bundled in a thick flannel coat and her neck wrapped in a scarf. She sits slumped with her arms folded and hands tucked under her armpits.

"Been here long?" he asks.

"Hour or so."

"Still hate me?"

She sits up straight. "Not really."

"What the fuck is the world coming to?" he says and it sounds just like he wants it to.

"It's come and gone, I think. It passed into Shitsville when we weren't looking."

They know better than to laugh but they do and it's as if this is the first joke they've ever shared. Like a long-forgotten memory. She moves closer to him and he puts his arm around her.

"You smell like a bottle," she says.

"But I'm okay. Where do we post tomorrow?"

"Nowhere. We're out of flyers. It'll be day after tomorrow before our next order is ready," she says, then she slides down and puts her head in his lap and feet up on the bench. The mist turns into a drizzle but the wind has died. She closes her eyes. Jon watches people walk back and forth in front of the Musée d'Orsay. They look up and around, cup their hands and peek into the lobby, tourists who believe museums keep minimart hours. A man and a woman without hats or umbrellas notice Jon and Estelle across the street on the bench and they hurry across the traffic and over to them. The man's face is smooth and slick in the rain and the woman hugs herself to keep warm. The man takes a tiny dictionary out of his pocket and fumbles through it but then gives up and he looks at Jon. The man points across the street at the museum and says slowly, "The mu-seum. O-pen? O-pen time?" And then he makes a motion with his hands as if he's opening a giant book.

Jon leans forward and says, "Go. The fuck. Away."

The man and woman look at each other, assuring themselves that this is what they have heard. Then they walk away along the sidewalk, looking back over their shoulders at the man who is staring.

"That was good," Estelle says.

Jon brushes the wet hair away from her face, touches the wrinkles in her forehead. He asks if she wants to get out of the weather but she says, "No. It feels good."

He lays his head back, listens to the traffic, listens to the river. The days, the weeks. Now the months. The accumulation is heavy and he is almost out when Estelle sits up and softly slaps his cheek.

"Wake up," she says. Her dark hair is flat on her head and she lick the moisture from her upper lip. "Let's go get drunk somewhere. Somewhere close before I change my mind."

"Fine," he says. "But I've got a head start."

"I'll catch you."

She stands, takes his hand, and pulls him to his feet. They walk back toward Saint-Michel, where they'll find a warm seat in a café at a table for two in a back corner. Where they'll spend more than they want to. Where they'll drink and smoke and throw out meaningless comments about the music or the waitress's shoes. Where they'll talk themselves into expectation.

2

Jon's mother was a thin, French-Swiss girl who moved to New York City when she was nineteen. She came to study dance but within a year she had married Jon's father, an all-American boy with a fullback's jaw. He was on the tail end of a modeling career and they scraped by in a three-room apartment in the city for several years. When she became pregnant with Jon, they moved back to the South to his father's hometown and his father ended up a branch manager of a bank.

While Jon was growing up, his mother taught him to speak French and she talked often of the small town she was from at the foot of the Alps. They would sit on the front porch swing and she would look across the treetops of the flat neighborhood and ask Jon to imagine mountaintops off in the distance, reaching into the clouds, littered with white no matter the season. She described a fresh snow, the purity of the river after a rain. She talked of train rides and of the smell of bread as you walked down the street. As he got older, he asked more questions, wondered why they never visited. She would only frown, then make up an excuse and laugh it off. But it was plenty to intrigue him and his second year of college he decided to study abroad in France to see if the things his mother had spoken of were true.

He studied in Blois, a busy town in the Loire Valley, an hour train ride from Paris. He had it better than the other American students because he spoke the language and he soon found himself irritated by their dependence on him as translator. So he avoided them, made time in the cafés and bars with the locals, made friends with the son of a vineyard owner, discovered the music, discovered the women. He wanted to give his time abroad more than a semester, and he needed to work to stay, so he took advantage of his Swiss citizenship and headed for Geneva. When he called home to give the news, his mother laughed and said, "So. You were listening." He heard his father moan in the background.

He found the Genevois predictable and tranquil and it was a good place to adapt, as the rituals of good food, good drink, less work were alive and enforced. He lived in a small room in a hostel and worked in a pub in the Old Town that was full of British and Irish expatriates. It was one of the few places in Geneva where night occasionally grew into morning and he had many drunk friends with thick accents who were easier to understand after four or five pints. But he found the pub to be too close to America and he'd walk by the cafés in the afternoons, see the same old men sitting in the same windows day after day, and he knew this is what his mother meant. So he quit the pub and found work at the Café Commerce, a small restaurant with only five bar stools and eight tables on the inside and four tables on the outside. He took a picture of it and mailed it to his mother.

The regulars asked him about America, about big cars and overtime. He exaggerated his replies, claimed his father worked sixty-five hours a week, that children were required to wear red, white, and blue to school every day. After a few months, Lucien, the café owner, gave him a raise and he moved out of the hostel and into four rooms above the café that Lucien's daughter was leaving to get married. In a few more months, as Lucien grew more comfortable with him, Jon was allowed to open and close, to hire and fire, to make recommendations for the plat du jour. He particularly liked the hiring, as waitresses came and went almost as often as customers. He had developed his father's simple good looks, a sharp brow and broad shoulders, and he did what any young man in a new country would do, he hired possibilities, which kept both him and the old men happy no matter how badly the service suffered.

After a year at the Café Commerce, he felt like he had been delivered to the kind of place that his mother had spoken about and it seemed as if he had always been there. He had realized since he first arrived in Blois that he wasn't going back to the place he had called home and it was time to call and explain. He knew his mother would understand. After he talked to her, she handed his father the phone and he explained again. "I'll be home for holidays and big deals," Jon said. His father took it the best he could and his mother swore they were coming to see him.

In the next year, he made two trips home. One trip had been for his mother's funeral. She had smoked right up until the time that she had to stay in the hospital and even then the nurses were constantly chasing after the cigarette smoke coming from her room. Jon had looked into the casket hoping for the stylish woman who had raised him to think past the city limits, but she wasn't there, only an elegant impression of her. Six months later his father passed away. Dropped dead in the tomato patch he had planted in the backyard, discovered by neighborhood kids chasing after their soccer ball. At his father's funeral he found himself wishing it would have been the other way around so that he could have brought his mother back with him to die in the place she belonged. After his father was in the ground, he returned to Geneva feeling more alone than he had before.

He spent more hours at work and the Café Commerce became his home, as he seldom wandered into the city. Never to the lake, never to the markets, never to the cinema. He would close the café at night, go upstairs to his apartment, then smoke cigarettes and have a few drinks and read and fall asleep on the couch. The morning would come and he would go down to the café, hours before anyone else arrived, have several espressos, smoke more cigarettes, read the paper. Then the help showed up, then the customers showed up, and before he knew it, he was sitting on the couch again.

Another year got away from him and one slow winter afternoon, the sun gone for weeks and business at a crawl, he sat on a bar stool in the quiet, the door closed to block out the street noise. He looked at his hands, looked at himself in the reflection of the café windows. He thought he was alone, then a man said in French from a back table, "You don't behave like a young man." Jon turned and the man was a regular, one of the old ones. The man had a thick white mustache and in the winter he kept a red scarf tied around his neck.

"I know," Jon answered. "I don't think this is the life she used to talk about."

"Who?" the man asked.

"My mother."

The next afternoon, he gave Lucien a month's notice. With Jon running the café, Lucien had found time for a girlfriend across the river in Carouge, and with a wife and three more daughters still at home, he agonized over having his afternoons again filled. Lucien offered him a raise, a better apartment, more liberty with the waitresses, but Jon declined. He spent the month saving every cent, selling furniture and clothes, sorting through what to keep and what to toss. He didn't like the boyish image on his Swiss passport, so he had a new one made. In the mornings, instead of reading the Geneva newspaper, he would walk to the newsstand at the train station and pick up a copy of *Le Figaro*, the Paris daily. Then he bought a pocket guide of Paris so he could get a grasp of the addresses of the apartments for rent, of the jobs offered. But he had never been to Paris, and while he understood it was a bigger, faster city than Geneva, the map overwhelmed him, an endless array of red, blue, yellow, and green lines that crossed and looped and crossed again. Which arrondissement is affordable? What addresses are near a metro line? What's a good neighborhood and what isn't and how long will it take to find work? He grew frustrated, timid. Wondered if he hadn't made a wrong decision. Two nights before he was to quit Geneva, he sat in his apartment repeating the same worries over and over until he got up from the couch, walked into the kitchen, and dropped the pocket guide in the garbage. The next morning he would ask for his job back.

He turned to the kitchen window and opened it and looked down into the street. The light of the tram shined blocks away and he watched it move in his direction, quiet people stepping in and out of the quiet tram in a quiet night. It approached his building and slid by, the click of the tracks no louder than a pencil tapping on a table. The air was cold and refreshing. A mother and a daughter walked along the sidewalk, the child singing a short, repetitive melody. The store windows of the street were dark.

And then he understood something about his father—why he was never interested in packing a bag, getting on a plane, and going somewhere where the people talked funny and he couldn't read the menu. He leaned out of the window, heard music coming from somewhere. He wondered how his mother felt about having never been back home and he wished he had sent her a plane ticket.

He walked to the garbage and picked out the Paris pocket guide. He flipped through it once more, then went into the bedroom and tossed it into a half-packed duffel bag. I'll figure it out when I get there, he thought. He took his American passport and dropped it in the garbage where the pocket guide had been. Then he went down to the café and sat in the shadows and drank a glass of wine to help him get to sleep.

A light snow fell on Geneva the morning Jon walked to the train station. He carried two duffel bags and in his coat pocket was his ticket, the morning copy of *Le Figaro*, and the pocket guide. The train was scheduled for 10:43 a.m. He was taking the TGV and in three hours he would be in Paris. He found the train on the departure board and walked to Voie 6. Passengers gathered and waited along the open corridor—men and women in business suits, mothers and daughters going shopping, a stray teenager here and there. The train was announced and in minutes it pulled into the station, silver and streamlined with a sharp orange streak running along its side. Jon found his car and climbed on with the other second classers. He put his bags in the luggage rack over the seat, sat down, took a deep breath. Others took off coats, pulled out magazines from purses and backpacks, put on headphones. Jon sat still with his arms folded, as if Paris were only around the corner.

The train sat for fifteen minutes as passengers boarded. Jon's seat was next to the window and he leaned against it, stared out at the people coming and going. He sat still, almost hypnotized, and was startled when the young woman with the heavy backpack fell into his lap.

"I'm sorry, I'm sorry," she apologized. "The bag made me fall." She spoke a quick French, the accent sharper than the French of Geneva. "It's okay," he said, and she pulled herself up. He stood and helped her lift the backpack into the overhead, then they both sat down.

"Books," she said. "Books that he never reads. My father sends me here twice a year to buy from my uncle's bookshop, though my uncle has never been to Paris to buy flowers. It's like a bag of stones." She spoke looking ahead, as if speaking into a mirror. "Next time say no, Estelle."

Jon smiled and looked once more out of the window. Unwrapping her scarf, she elbowed him in the side of the head. He grimaced and she apologized again.

"I'm Jon," he said.

"I'm Estelle."

"I know. I was listening before. Why would your uncle need to buy flowers in Paris?"

"It doesn't matter," she said, and she sat back, looking mildly embarrassed. Her brown hair flipped up around the collar of her coat and her eyes were green like limes. The tip of her nose was still red from the cold.

"You're an American," she said. "I can tell from the accent. So many Americans in Paris, they have their own sound."

"I was. American, I mean. But not anymore."

"Then what are you?"

He shrugged. "I'm not sure. In three hours, I guess Parisian."

"Are you moving there?"

"For now. I don't know if I'll stay."

She smiled. "You'll stay. At least for a while. It's difficult to leave."

"Well. I hope."

"Only remember that the cold does not last forever."

"I'll remember."

"How is your head?"

He touched it and felt the tender spot. "It's good."

A whistle sounded and the train doors closed. The train eased forward. People who had been whispering as the train sat still began to talk. Estelle pushed a button on the armrest and leaned her seat back. The train station moved by slowly in the window and, once clear, the train gathered speed and Geneva passed by faster and faster. Jon watched as the city blocks disappeared, as the neighborhoods disappeared, and the train became a bullet shooting out of Switzerland and across the snow-scattered farmlands of France. He looked at Estelle and her eyes were closed and her hands folded in her lap. A strand of hair had fallen across her cheek. She stuck out her bottom lip and tried to blow the hair away but it didn't move. Jon reached over and moved it from her face. She opened her eyes and said, "Thank you."

Halfway to Paris, Estelle admitted she spoke English, though not very well. She asked him to speak it to help her practice. He found out that she and her family had lived in Paris her entire life, that she was an only child, that she spent a month in London one summer but had never been to the States. Her family owned several flower shops in different parts of the city. He explained his Swiss mother and that though he had spent a semester in Blois, he'd never taken the trip to Paris.

"Why are you going now?" she asked.

"I could have gone south to Italy but I don't speak Italian. Germany is no good. No Spain for the same reason no Italy. I need to be somewhere that I can speak so I can get a job."

"Paris is much different than Geneva."

"That's what I'm hoping."

"But the best thing to do is find a neighborhood. If you find a neighborhood that you like, then sometimes you forget that Paris is so big."

"Okay," he said, and he pulled out the pocket guide. He pointed and asked questions about neighborhoods and she would put her finger to her chin, think for a moment, then answer. She frowned on some of the arrondissements, mentioning things like too many old people or not enough metros and Jon scribbled question marks on top of these. Some she smiled at, the ones she liked, named the good restaurants and shops and shady park benches. He asked where he could find the most cafés and she told him that anywhere close to the river would be a good place to look for work.

"If you would like, when we arrive, I will take you to a street close to where I work where there are many inexpensive hotels. Not so fancy, maybe."

"You don't have to do that."

"Okay. Whatever you like."

"But maybe I can help with the giant bag. And we would be even."

"The bag," she said, rolling her eyes. "I forgot about the bag."

They arrived at the Gare d'Austerlitz and Jon bought a luggage roller for her backpack, ignoring the money she tried to put in his hand as he paid for it. They exited the station and walked through Jardin des Plantes and its wide, pebbled pathways. Despite the cold, women pushed children in strollers, curious eyes peeking out between scarves and sock hats. Old men sat on the park benches reading the newspaper. The trees were bare and thick. They came to the Quai Saint-Bernard and walked along the river. Estelle walked ahead as Jon was slower with his duffel bags and he kept stopping to look around. She would look over her shoulder every few steps to make sure he was still there. They continued along the river until the Île de la Cité was in sight and he recognized Notre-Dame from pictures. Estelle said, "You won't find anything cheap in that direction." She turned left, away from the river and the sights, onto rue Saint-Jacques. The street ran uphill and she pointed and said, "Go this way. Once you get to the top of the hill you will see many small hotels."

He put down his bags and said, "What does Estelle do on the days that she is not traveling to Geneva for her father?"

"Estelle helps her father with the business."

Jon looked away from her and up the hill. "I was thinking that maybe tomorrow you could show me where to eat lunch. If you can get away from work again."

She nodded, her nose and cheeks red from the cold. "Yes, but only because you bought me these wheels for the backpack."

"Can I call you after I find a place?"

"No," she said. "Meet me here tomorrow. Right on this spot. At midday."

"Midday," Jon said, and he leaned to her and they exchanged two kisses and then he gave her a third.

"Not anymore," she said. "Only three in Geneva. In Paris, we give two. You need to start thinking like a Parisian."

"I'll remember," he said, and she turned and walked away from him, and when she turned the corner, he kicked himself for not getting a number, an address, something. Though he knew that if she didn't return to this spot tomorrow, a phone number would be of no good anyway.

He found the Hôtel de Medicis, simple and small and easy on the budget. His room was on the fourth floor and he could stand in the middle, stretch out his arms, and nearly touch all four walls. The window opened onto a mini-balcony and he stepped outside. There was a chair and a terra-cotta pot was filled with cigarette butts and a copy of *L'Étranger* had been left behind in the chair. Across the street was a lamb kabob stand, a fruit and vegetable grocery, a flower shop. He wondered if it was Estelle's. From somewhere he heard an old man's voice singing. Scooters and pint-size cars zipped down the narrow street. He hoped it would snow.

He barely slept. The thin mattress sagged with his weight and he kept dreaming he was in his warm bedroom in Geneva, only to wake to hear footsteps up and down the staircase. He woke early and walked. Shop owners sprayed sidewalks and men in green jumpsuits picked up the garbage. There was no snow but a light mist. He stopped three times for coffee, each time measuring the café to see if it was a place he might want to work and each time leaving uninterested. He walked through the Latin Quarter and so many signs written in English helped him realize that he didn't want to work there, so he made his way up the river and as he walked he forgot about finding a job and he forgot about finding a place to live as he soaked in the flow of the river and the hustle of the traffic and the detail of the architecture. He paused at a couple of book stands but didn't linger long as he wanted to keep walking, keep watching. Closer to noon the sun fought its way through the clouds for an instant and shined a fresh light on the city and added a pep to Jon's walk. It was then that he realized that he wasn't sure how far he was from the street corner where he was to meet Estelle and he looked at his watch and it was ten minutes until noon. He traced his steps back along the river, back through the Quarter, back toward the hotel, and back down the hill and he arrived five minutes late. He waited and watched in all directions. Another five minutes passed and he told himself he would give her another five. Another five came and went and he gave her another five. And as those five disappeared he told himself to shrug it off, that there were millions of other people in the city waiting to meet him, and he shoved his hands in his pockets and started across the street toward a newspaper stand and that was when he saw her coming toward him with a blue scarf wrapped around her neck.

◣

They ate lunch at a café on the rue Saint-Jacques and in the afternoon she taught him the metro. The day after she took him through the Gardens of Luxembourg and the Tuileries. And so on and so on, day after day, until the city and Estelle merged into the same experience, one as new and intimidating and hopeful as the other.

He found a three-room apartment and took a job in a trendy café in Saint-Sulpice that opened early and closed late and gave him a look at the women with the sleek hips at night and the men with the newspapers and cigars in the morning. Estelle would come and sit in the café at night, sometimes with friends and sometimes alone, and he would pass by her table each trip around the floor, touching her shoulder or lighting her cigarette or sometimes sitting down and staring as if she were a work of art. She often stayed until he closed the café and walked home with him and spent the night with him and he would leave her asleep the next morning as he left early and she never seemed to have to be anywhere. A benefit of being a daughter working for my father, she had said when he commented on her leisurely schedule.

"But it won't last forever," she said. "Spring is almost here."

When spring arrived, the flower shops boomed and the tables turned. Jon spent his few free hours in the afternoon chasing after her as she crisscrossed the city tending to the family shops, and he not only was introduced to the serious side of Estelle, but also to her serious but good-hearted father and her blue-eyed mother whose eyeglasses always sat on top of her head. The spring turned into the summer and on his days off he helped out in the shops, working in the back, Estelle's mother teaching him how to cut and trim and set a bouquet and her father taking Jon along on big deliveries to graveyards and wedding receptions. Estelle made fun of him, warning that the only reason her parents liked him was because he gave them free labor. And lying in bed one night in his apartment, after she had waited on him to close up the café, he joked back that free labor was a small offering in exchange for their only daughter.

He had meant to do it but he hadn't meant to do it like that. But it had come out and she sat up in the bed and said, "What does that mean?"

"You know what it means," he said. "Are you brave enough to marry me?"

"Let's see who is the brave one," she smiled and said, and she made him get up and get dressed and they took a taxi across the city in the middle of the night to her parents' apartment. She had a key but instead she knocked and knocked on the door until her father opened it and he stood there in his robe.

"Okay," Estelle said to Jon. "Tell him what you asked me."

"You'll pay for this," he answered. Then he took a deep breath and told her father that he wanted to marry his daughter. Her father told them to wait and he closed the door. When it opened again, her mother was there with her father.

"Start again," her father said.

Jon looked at Estelle and said, "Yes. I am the brave one." Then he told her parents that he wanted to marry Estelle and that after all this, he fully expected everyone to agree.

At the beginning of autumn, as the breeze cooled and the blooms began to hide away for another year, Jon and Estelle stood together in front of a priest in a four-hundred-year-old cathedral along the Seine, white rose petals from a family store tossed into the aisle, smiles on both of their faces.

They honeymooned in the south. Saint-Tropez. A tiny village made for millionaires and beautiful children, yachts in the harbor, sunshine almost touchable. They had a quaint hotel room over a café with windows that looked into the harbor, small and semicircled, and bars and restaurants surrounding it. Sunglasses on everyone, even into the evening, and the smell of baking bread creeping into the open windows of the room in the early morning.

Around the turn of the harbor and into the rocks and behind the lighthouse was a bench. They sat there at night and the wind blew in their faces and across the bay the white lights of the houses and villas shined like new answers. A slapping of the water on the rocks, an easy beating. Stars scattered in the sky like a handful of salt tossed across a puddle of oil. Her head in his lap. No words. They woke up and couldn't believe they had fallen asleep, then couldn't think of a better place *to* fall asleep and the sun was coming up, and the sky was a deep blue, so true across the horizon that it was hard to tell where the sky stopped and the water began. Jon offered to get espresso and left her lying stretched out across the bench, the curve in her hip as beautiful as any eastern glow.

Steps away from her, it started to push him, that same feeling that came over him the last days in Geneva, that perfect loneliness, safe and unflinching. It came hard, shoving into his back and between his shoulder blades and then right through the top of his head, and he believed it, listened to it, agreed when it said that from here on there is not only love but the responsibility of being two together and he walked into the harbor, past the early morning cafés.

But he didn't let it win. He shoved back and told it that those days were over as he imagined the way that her hair was brushed away from her neck as she lay with her hands folded under her head. The day was slowly growing brighter, breaking from the softness of a heavier light, as long white birds were diving for breakfast. In the sky the moon lingered, not ready to give in to morning, and he kept walking and kept pushing the solitude to the back of his mind until he was confident that he had won and the walk felt something like a victory lap.

Moments later, he sat down next to her, rubbed her back until she woke. She sat up, yawned and stretched, saw the espresso and chocolate croissants, and she couldn't believe she had fallen back asleep so easily and they sat quietly with each other until the sun sat on the horizon.

3

He often thinks about the night in Saint-Tropez when he left Estelle asleep. And he remembers it now as he looks across the table at her in an Italian restaurant. Marinara sauce drips from her chin when she takes a large bite. He points and she wipes her mouth and says, "Why aren't you eating?"

"I am. It's good," he says.

The sun shines and there has been talk of an early spring but that talk arrives every year—the first glint of sun, the first dry week, and hope for the new season begins. A couple sits at a table outside and they watch them through the window.

"Look at her," Estelle says. "She's shivering. And he's sitting on his hands. They never learn."

"I think you should write a book about Paris. *The Truth*, you could call it."

"No one would read it. No one wants the truth."

"Then we could name it *My Beautiful Paris* and trick people into the truth whether they want it or not."

Estelle pours herself more wine from the carafe and says, "That's the only way."

Month four. Second week. Jon has a week's vacation beginning tomorrow and they will make another loop around Paris with new, full-color folding pamphlets and two-by-three-foot posters to replace the flyers. The cost of the high-gloss paper and the posters has nearly wiped out what remains of their savings. It will be a hurried week and late last night Estelle suggested, to Jon's surprise, that before it begins, they should spend Sunday out of the apartment, away from the telephone that doesn't ring, away from the television without news. Her rule: not a word about you know what.

They woke early, dressed warmly, and walked three blocks to their favorite bakery. The owner, a short, plump woman with dyed black hair, said she was happy to see them again. She asked about Jennifer but Estelle only shook her head. The woman wouldn't let them have croissants from the basket on the shelf but instead made them wait on hot ones from the oven. She brought them another coffee when the first was gone. When they stood up to leave, she wouldn't let them pay.

They took the metro to rue Saint-Germain and to a string of book-stores, used paperbacks covering large tables along the sidewalk. It was early still and easy to browse. By the last bookstore they had bought six novels that they knew would never be read. The streets weren't crowded and they continued slowly along the sidewalk, pausing to look in store windows at shoes and coats. Jon bought cigarettes at a magazine kiosk and offered one to Estelle but she declined and left Jon outside to smoke as she went into a hip clothing store for teenagers. He only smoked half the cigarette and then he followed after her. She went to the racks of jeans and pulled out a pair of dark denim, low-waist jeans. She held them to Jon and said, "I bet I could fit nicely into these with a little more walking." Jon nodded, hoping the same thing. Estelle finished browsing and they moved along to a frame shop and then a pottery store, never buying, only picking up items they liked, showing them to each other, and moving on.

Then they walked. The sun shined but the wind remained cool. They came to the river and walked past the outdoor vendors selling vin-tage magazines, prints of the city, LPs, silver jewelry. More people emp-tied into the streets in the late morning. They left the river and walked until they stumbled upon an empty playground and they sat down on a bench and watched the birds peck in the sand. A father with two small boys came to the playground and they got up and left. Estelle suggested Italian for lunch and Jon suggested a couple of places but it meant getting on the metro and they were avoiding the metro. So they kept walking. Jon said, "Maybe we'll get lucky." And they did, finding an Italian eatery on a quiet corner, not another restaurant on the block. The meal had been good and now the wine warms them as Estelle continues to poke fun at the couple sitting outside.

"What's next?" Jon asks and takes out cigarettes. They each take one and Estelle says, "A movie?"

"Sounds good. How about another carafe first?" She nods and Jon lifts the empty carafe to the waiter, who quickly brings another.

When the wine is finished, they stand, both lighter than before. They walk until Jon waves down a taxi and it takes them to Odéon. The sun shines full on the early afternoon and Estelle opens the buttons on her coat. The narrow square at Odéon is busy with people in and out of the metro and groups gather and talk with their hands in their pockets. Some walk with bicycles and some walk with dogs and some stand alone and turn in a circle, wondering if they are early or late. Several cinemas surround the square, flanked by sandwich shops and walk-in cafés. Jon and Estelle join the others who stroll from cinema to cinema and skim the movies and times.

"Do you have a preference?" he asks.

"Something that doesn't require thinking. How about one of those action films with lots of explosions?"

Jon has seen the previews to a film titled *ProActive* and plane crashes and a burning White House flash in his mind. Estelle nods okay and they get tickets, then popcorn, and they sit in the back of the theater.

In the opening scene, a good-looking cop in the streets of Washington, D.C., manages to chase down, on foot, an SUV filled with Eastern European spies. The cop shoots the tires and the SUV does two somersaults through an intersection. Then the bad guys, unfazed, jump out of the burning car with their guns blazing but are cut down by the handsome man who has barely broken a sweat in the D.C. afternoon.

After the scene, Estelle slumps in her chair, squeezes Jon's arm, and whispers, "Good choice."

It's two hours of quiet between them. Two hours in the dark without imagining. Two hours of good conquering evil, no matter how many bullets or bodies it takes. The film ends with the hero sitting on the lawn of the charred White House, fire engines and high arches of water in the background, the president's hand on his shoulder, certain they have rid the world of what ails it. The sparse crowd empties out of the theater but Jon and Estelle sit still as the credits roll, then the screen goes blank and the low lights of the theater are turned on. Jon looks over and Estelle is asleep, her body turned to the side, her hands together as if praying, tucked under her cheek.

Her mouth is slightly open and she breathes deeply. He looks at the screen and it is gray in the low light. Two teenagers in black pants and white shirts come in with brooms and garbage bags and begin to clean the aisles.

Almost five months, he thinks. And then he prays that if the end is going to be bad, at least give her back so we can have a funeral.

Estelle shifts but doesn't wake and he looks at her. He remembers the clarity of her face the day he met her on the train, full of answers, full of everything that could be good about a train ride. The days and weeks and months learning Paris, learning her. Her pregnant belly, her lust for a cigarette during the final weeks, the green eyes of the baby. And then he can't remember anymore, his mind drawing a nine-year blank.

Estelle shifts again and this time she wakes. She sits up, stretches, wipes her mouth. "Good morning," Jon says.

"How long did you let me sleep?" she asks and falls over into his lap.

"Not long. I'm guessing you missed the big ending. America was saved again."

"Maybe that's what I need to listen to at night to sleep, gunfire and bad dialogue."

"We'll rent some movies on the way home."

Outside, it is twilight and cooler than before. Jon hails a taxi, and as it gets close to their neighborhood, Estelle says, "Let's walk some more." She asks the driver to take them to Luxembourg. The park is nearly empty and the evening grows dark quickly, like a stage after the final scene. They walk around a fountain that is turned off and the water sits still like a pond. Waiters from the outdoor cafés turn up chairs onto tables. At the gates which open into the Place de l'Odéon, they pass two old women pushing two grocery carts filled with dirty clothes and shoes. One of the women holds an empty paper cup toward Jon and he gives her the change in his pocket. The other woman asks for a cigarette and he gives her five. Cars pass through the intersection lethargically, without the hum and hustle of midday, and across the street from the park gate, two policemen stand in front of a restaurant and talk with its animated owner.

Along Saint-Germain the stores remain open and the window lights illuminate the sidewalks. Shopkeepers stand in the doorways, their arms folded, ready to go home. Jon and Estelle turn left at rue Saint-Jacques and walk toward the river and when Estelle feels a raindrop she says, "Let's go home."

He asks if she's hungry but she says no and they stop at the Quai Saint-Michel to wave a taxi. Cameras flash across the bridge as the lights of Notre-Dame glow orange in the dark sky. A guided group of Japanese tourists approach and swallow Estelle and Jon. He takes Estelle's hand and tries to step out of their way but there are at least seventy-five of them, chatting and aiming their cameras and unaware that other people are on the street. Over their heads Jon sees taxis passing and tries to wave but the taxis speed by. The street sign says "Don't walk" and the group stops, Jon and Estelle caught inside. Goddammit," Jon says and clenches his jaw.

Estelle says, "Calm down," but Jon squeezes her hand tighter and pushes through the small crowd with his forearm, the Japanese calling him names he can't understand.

"It's just a church! You've never seen a church before?" he yells at them when he and Estelle are free. A few of the men shout back in quick vowels and then over their shouts and over the hum of passing cars, Jon thinks he hears a voice call, "Daddy!"

"Did you hear that?" he asks Estelle.

She looks around. "Hear what?"

"Listen." He holds his finger to her mouth. Looks up and down the street. Hears it again. Then he sees a brown-haired girl and a woman in a business suit crawl into a taxi half a block away.

"It's Jennifer," he says and takes off running for the taxi. *Arrêtez! Arrêtez!* he yells, the brake lights shining red as the taxi sits still. Estelle runs behind him and calls out but he doesn't listen and he is twenty feet from the taxi when the brake lights disappear and it moves into traffic. He runs behind, reaching out, the taxi trunk barely out of his reach. The taxi speeds and he looks into the backseat and the girl turns and half waves at Jon. "Goddammit! Stop!" he screams again, and lunges out once more and he loses his balance and falls forward, banging his elbows and knees on the asphalt. The taxi pulls away, the driver not noticing the man running and screaming behind them.

Estelle catches up, finds Jon lying on his back in the middle of the street. She turns and faces the traffic and waves several cars around. The light at the end of the block turns red and the traffic pauses. She kneels beside him and says, "What are you doing? Are you okay?"

He rolls over, gets on all fours, and crawls to the sidewalk. She sits down beside him. "What was it? Was it her?" she asks, and he knows that she only asks to appease him, in the way that she let him run and believe.

He shakes his head, leans back, and rests on his elbows. "We're not supposed to talk about it today."

Estelle takes a deep breath and her eyes water. The light changes and cars again move down the street. "Do you want me to wave the taxi?" she asks, and he shakes his head. "I don't care," he says.

She pulls her collar up around her neck. Does the same for him. He doesn't move. She moves parallel to him and leans on her elbows and they are twins stretched out on the sidewalk, her legs nearly as long as his. They stare into the sky and the chimes of Notre-Dame resonate in deep, throbbing tones. Several of the Japanese tourists who have watched the action sneak along the sidewalk closer to them, take their picture, then hurry away.

4

It rains the next three days as Jon moves constantly around the city handing out the new pamphlets in the metro, outside government buildings, on the outskirts of the city where rents are low. He places the new posters in metro halls, at the train stations, on public notice boards in the parks. Jennifer's face is clear in the full-color photograph, her smile shows her teeth, her hair in a ponytail. Detective Marceau suggested a photo with her hair pulled back to focus on the face.

The rain has been steady and he has been wet from morning until returning home in the evening. Estelle has caught a second wind and she sits in the apartment and plots the strategy with a revived gusto. On Monday morning she threw away the worn, smaller maps and she bought new red pens, a poster-size city map, and a carton of cigarettes. She removed photographs and a shelf from a kitchen wall and put the map up with nails. She uses a yellow highlighter to mark the areas less likely to prove helpful, tourist spots and business centers where people hurry. At the end of each day Jon comes home, sits in a hot bath, tells her he had a good day.

When Jon leaves the apartment Thursday morning, the rain has stopped but the clouds remain. Over his shoulder is a duffel bag filled with the pamphlets. He carries the posters in a plastic tube. He is bound for the northern part of the city, to the eighteenth arrondissement. He stops at M. Conrer's café and has two coffees and a short glass of whiskey. M. Conrer says *"Bonne chance"* as he walks out the door.

He gets on the metro and sits down. He has twelve stops to wait. By the time the metro reaches Abbesses there is no crowd, only a handful of people getting on and off. He walks to both exits and puts up new posters, and on an earlier orange poster, a black question mark has been drawn in the center of Jennifer's face. He doesn't remember if he did it or not.

He walks up the stairs of the exit and the streets are more quiet here than in the city's center. Half the stores have yet to open, trucks deliver newspapers to the newsstands, a dog without an owner walks by Jon as he kneels to reach into the duffel bag for pamphlets. At the end of the street is a bus stop and, not yet ready to begin, he walks over and sits down. He opens the pamphlet.

Inside is Jennifer's birth date, ID number, height, weight, hair and eye color. The mention of a mole on the right shoulder. Unique traits: she bites her bottom lip, left-handed, bony elbows and knees, speaks French, English, and very basic Italian. When and where she was last seen. What she was wearing. The name of the school she attends and its phone number. Detective Marceau's contact information. A phone number for Estelle at home. A phone number for Jon at work. Then at the bottom of the right side, in bold black lettering, the reward of fifty thousand euros. No one is sure where it will come from.

There's too goddamn much on here, he thinks. Or maybe not enough.

A bus arrives and opens its doors. Jon climbs the bus steps, hands the driver the pamphlet, then gets off and sits down on the bench again. The dog that passed him before returns and sits at his feet. Its tongue hangs out, pink and dry, and its coat is reddish-brown, but the nose is white. It has a collar and Jon looks at the tag, but the tag is scratched and faded and unreadable.

"I don't know what to tell you," he says and the dog leaves. Jon watches it walk into the open door of a café. He sits until another bus arrives but he only waves it on when the door opens. He takes flyers from the duffel bag, leaves them on the bench, then goes into the same café as the dog.

The dog lies on the floor at the end of the bar, a bowl of water and a bowl of food next to it. Jon sits at a table against the wall and sets the duffel bag in the chair across from him. He lays the tube on the table. A teenage girl in a crimson turtleneck and jeans comes over and asks what he'd like. He asks for another coffee and another whiskey, then he takes off his coat and takes the morning paper from the table next to him. The waitress returns and he decides to drink before reading. He looks around the café, at the dog, at the young girl, then on the wall across from him he notices a painting.

She is in front of the waterfall, the sun behind her. Her dress is thin and hangs like a slip and rises above her knees. Her skin is rich and chocolate and her bare feet are crossed as she leans with her back against a rock as tall as she is. She tilts her head forward and toward the ground and her black hair is long and straight and falls to the front, and with the light behind her, her face is draped in shadow, her eyes dead set like stones. The shadow breaks across her chest and soft light shines on her arms and legs.

Jon crosses the room to look closer. "Do you know who painted this?" he asks the waitress.

"I think Iris. Iris something."

"Can you find out for sure?"

She shrugs her shoulders and says, "I'll have to ask my father." Jon looks back at the painting and tries to think of a name for her, something exotic, strange. Something with –asia on the end. The girl goes through a swinging door into the kitchen and Jon hears her ask the father about the artist. She returns and walks around the bar to Jon, then hands him a slip of paper. "This is her name," she says. "Her studio is close to here. Four or five blocks."

He reads the name. Iris Conrad, 82 rue Tholoz. After the coffee and whiskey he leaves money on the table and walks out of the café. The wind blows and pushes the clouds and by afternoon there might be sun. Shop owners move tables onto the sidewalks. A group of schoolchildren in navy-blue sweaters cross the street in single file like a row of ducks as a large woman with glasses and an even larger navy-blue sweater directs. Jon makes it three blocks, then at the fourth he comes to rue Tholoz, a narrow, one-way brick street lined by four-story buildings. Puddles linger from three days' rain and stretch the length of the curb and a truck blocks the street as two men load furniture into the back of it. He finds the address and the building is more worn than the others, its faded beige stucco cracked and missing both high and low, exposing pockets of red brick and crumbling mortar. The nameplate is there and he goes into the unlocked front door of the building. The stairway is dimly lit and he climbs to the third floor, stepping lightly, as if trying to sneak in and out undetected. On the third floor there is only one door and he knocks.

A voice from inside calls softly, "Who is it?"

Jon hesitates, hasn't thought of what he would say. She calls out again, and he answers, "Excuse me but I'm looking for Iris Conrad. I saw some of your work and liked it. Is that you?"

She's quiet.

"Please, just give me a minute to talk with you." The lock clicks and the door opens.

"Only a moment," she says. "I am working and it's hard to start back again if I wait too long."

He steps inside and the strong, toxic smell of paint makes him momentarily light-headed. He follows her into a large room without furniture, painting after painting of women, leaning on the walls and sitting on easels. Drop cloths cover the floor from wall to wall. The walls are brick and splattered with an array of colors as if a child has been allowed to play. Two tall windows look out across a small courtyard, no larger than the room itself.

She walks into the middle of the room, turns, props her hands on her hips. Jon sets the duffel bag and poster tube on the floor. "You have so many," he says.

She only nods and moves toward the windows, folds her arms. Her hair is auburn and choppy and looks like she cuts it herself. Her face is fair and her mouth small, and her lips shine as if wet. She wears a splattered T-shirt and baggy jeans rolled up to her knees and she's barefoot, her feet and calves spotted with blue and white paint. She unfolds her arms and turns to Jon and she is as old as he is, maybe older.

"What do you want?" she asks, and her French has a distinct German accent.

He looks around the room, and says, "All women?"

"You walked all the way down this dirty street to tell me this? If you're finished, I need to get back to work. I'm not a child with finger paint."

Jon looks at two paintings side by side on easels. In the first, a woman sits on a park bench with her legs stretched out and her arms to her sides as if she is unconscious or sleeping. In the second, a woman, dressed in nearly nothing, is sitting on concrete steps, the building unseen. In each painting, and in all of the different paintings in the room, the expression of the faces is long and melancholy, like the painting in the café.

"I saw one of your paintings in a café a few blocks from here. A woman in front of a waterfall," Jon says as he kneels down and looks at a woman reflected in a store window. "Why not men?"

She gives a playful laugh, then says, "What is mysterious about the man?"

He thinks. Looks down. Can't answer.

"I look at you now and you are as blank as a bed sheet," she says. "A man is a marquee, bright and obvious. A woman is la mer. Always the face of the woman is the man's answer to everything. Like in life. If a woman smiles, the man thinks he has done well. If she frowns, he believes he has done wrong. It is not so simple."

"Do you know what painting I'm talking about in the café?"

She walks around Jon, circles the room with her hands behind her back, hums a solid note. He notices her forearms and calves, thin and pale like sand.

"Yes, I remember this. A scared woman."

"She was scared?"

"Then—yes. Now—I don't know. What did you see when you looked at her?"

"Lost, I think. Or waiting on someone."

She rubs her forehead and brushes back her hair, then points at a portrait of a woman sitting in a chair with a book. "And this one. What do you see?"

Her legs are apart and her elbows rest on the chair arms. The head is turned away from the open book. "She doesn't look comfortable. Maybe she is doing something she shouldn't. Surprised, I think."

Out of the corner of his eye, he sees her head nod.

"Is that right?" he asks.

She shrugs. "How do I know? I only paint them because they keep me company. It is up to you what you see."

"I don't know what I see. Nothing."

"No. I don't think you see nothing."

I see nothing very clearly, he thinks. More clearly every day.

She looks over her shoulder at the duffel bag and says, "What is in the bag?"

"Nothing," he says.

She laughs, says, "You are full of nothing."

"I told you."

They exchange a smile and the moment stalls. He folds his arms, looks away from her. "Do you sell your work?" he asks.

She shrugs her shoulders. "Sometimes. If I need to. But it is difficult to let them go. They take time."

"Would you sell the woman in the café?"

"That's a question for the café. They already bought it. Why do you want her?"

"I don't know. She reminds me of someone."

He looks at Iris and feels himself drift. He looks at her but looks through her, as if she were made of mesh. I want her because she reminds me of someone. Because I think she is waiting and I don't want her to wait any longer. And then he closes his eyes and when he opens them they are full and he bites down to hold the tears back but they escape. "I'm sorry for bothering you," he says and she steps to him. She takes the front of her shirt and reaches up to his face and wipes it. She is half a foot shorter than him and the shirt lifts high and she is exposed, the skin of her stomach and breasts the same soothing pale tone, and Jon notices a coin-size tattoo of a star between her breasts. And then something else in him moves, pushing down the hurt. Iris steps back and continues to hold the sweatshirt up above her stomach. He looks down her neck, to her stomach and then to her feet, and she says, "Maybe you are not so obvious."

"Can I show you something?" he asks. She nods and Jon picks up the tube and takes out a poster, unfolds it, and shows it to Iris. "This is my daughter," he says.

She looks up and down the poster, reaches for it, but her fingertips stop short of touching the child's face. "How long?" she asks.

"About five months. Forever."

I have to go, he thinks as he looks at Jennifer. I have work to do. I have to go. He rolls the poster and says, "If I leave this, will you paint her like you have painted the others?"

She pauses and looks toward the window. "No," she says.

"Why not?"

"It's not something I want to do."

"But why?"

"Because she is real. These paintings aren't real. If I paint her she won't look the way that she looks. She will be different."

"I don't care. It's something."

"But I don't want to."

"I'll pay you."

"That doesn't matter."

"No shit," he says. "I've been trying to pay people for five months to help, and you're right, it doesn't matter." He opens the tube and sticks the poster inside and then he grabs the duffel bag.

"Slow down," she says and she grabs his arm. "Your eyes are still wet." She takes the duffel bag from his hand and sets it down, and then she takes away the tube, and then she rubs her hands slowly up and down his arms as if to smooth the fabric. He stands still, feels something move again in the way that she touches him. She raises her shirt to wipe his face and the star reappears.

"Do you have anything to drink?" he asks.

She nods and says, "Some wine." But Jon doesn't let her walk away. Instead, he reaches out and takes her shirt in his hands and slowly eases it up. She surprises him when she lifts her arms and he pulls it over her head and the feeling shoots through him that if he could only take her jeans off and lay her down and spread her legs then the world would stop and give him a moment's peace. The feeling shoots through him like an arrow. It owes me, he thinks. Doesn't matter who I am and who she is. It owes me this. This thoughtless act. One thoughtless act. Just close your eyes and fuck it all away. Estelle can blame me but would she, and if I could give her a moment, wouldn't I? Iris unbuttons his coat and he lets it drop from his shoulders and to the floor. He wants to say something but doesn't know what and then his shirt is gone and she is stepping out of the jeans that have fallen around her ankles and he stares at the star and she unbuckles his belt. They stand there, facing each other, naked except for what is necessary, still covered by soft material.

If I could give her a moment, wouldn't I? He thinks of her, curled on the couch in the middle of the night, eyes held open by question marks. He gets on his knees and runs his hands along the hips of the woman who paints the empty expressions, slips his fingers inside her panties. Pulling them down would be as easy as a breath but he holds. She runs her hand sympathetically across the top of his head.

He removes his fingers. Slides his hands down the sides of her legs, touches the spots of paint on her feet. He reaches over and picks up her shirt from the floor and holds it to her. She takes it and he starts to apologize then he wonders what the hell for, all I want is a goddamn moment of peace and what am I apologizing for, and he snatches the sweatshirt from her and he pulls her down and there is no more stopping and she is warm and the perfect center of nothing.

He wakes and finds her beside him. A white sheet covers them. He looks around at the paintings and the women stare back. Iris has her back turned to him. Dull afternoon light shines in the windows, the sun still hidden by clouds. He slides out from under the blanket and picks up his clothes. As he is dressing, she wakes and sits up. She covers herself with the sheet and watches him step into his pants, then she stretches and the sheet falls. She yawns, then says, "There is a bottle of wine in the kitchen. Through that door. Bring it for us."

"I can't. Not now."

She frowns, then says, "What a strange first day for us."

The first day, he thinks, and feels an odd comfort that she has made this sound like a beginning.

He doesn't look at her, doesn't look at the paintings, but stares at the wall.

"Every day is strange," he says. "And tomorrow will be stranger than today." He picks up the tube and the bag. "I'm supposed to be putting these up around the city. I have to go."

"Can I keep one?" she asks.

"I thought you said no."

"I did say no. And I still mean no. But if you don't leave one, there is no chance."

Jon opens the tube and sets a poster on the floor. "Do you paint every day?" he asks.

"I am here all the time," she says and she stands without the sheet. She takes his arm and walks him to the door. "You can come back if you would like."

Jon takes another long look at her body, at the tattoo, then he opens the door and she stands behind it, hiding herself from any eyes in the hallway.

◂

After Iris closes the door, she listens to make certain Jon is out of the building. Then she gets dressed and sits in the floor and unrolls the poster of Jennifer. She admires the child's cheekbones, the innocent skin, the arched eyebrows. She goes into the kitchen and from the garbage she takes two empty water bottles and two empty wine bottles and sets them on the edges of the poster. Then she removes a painting near the window from its easel and she takes the easel and a clean canvas into another empty room of the apartment. She sits again on the floor and stares at Jennifer. After several minutes, she stands, walks slowly around the room, watching the child's face change with the shifting glare of the daylight, with the shadow of her body as she crosses in front of the window. She circles twice, then she sits again and rips the contact information off the bottom of the poster, leaving only the child.

She gets up and takes the empty bottles and poster into the other room. She spreads the child out on the floor next to the easel, goes back for the paint and brushes. She looks on the floor at Jennifer and then she thinks of Jon. His blank face propped on top of broad, sagging shoulders. And then she dabs her brush into the black and makes two dots where she believes the eyes will be. She stands back and the dots appear heavy and cold, but she likes it, and thinks it appropriate for this new work to begin with the emptiness.

5

It is dark by the time Jon reaches his street and he avoids M. Conrer's and goes upstairs. Estelle is gone, a note next to the telephone saying she is at the grocery. He goes into the kitchen and pours a glass of water, then takes a black marker and puts an X on the map across the eighteenth arrondissement.

He drinks the water, then goes into the shower. He takes the water as hot as he can stand it, leaning his head forward and allowing the stream to run on his neck and down his back. He looks at his hands. Feels as though there should be dirt under his fingernails. After the shower he puts on a robe and goes into the bedroom and lies on the bed. He turns on the television to watch the news but the evening edition is over and he will have to wait until eleven o'clock. The apartment door opens and he turns off the television, rolls on his stomach, and pretends to be asleep.

Estelle comes in with her arms filled with plastic grocery bags. She puts the groceries away, unaware Jon is in the apartment until she sees the X on the map. She calls for him but he doesn't answer. She looks in the bathroom and the shower curtain is wet, then she goes into the bedroom, notices his eyes closed, and she sits down beside him and puts her hand on his back.

When Jon's father passed away, he inherited little, but included in a box his mother had prepared for him was his father's portfolio from the modeling years. It was three inches thick of his handsome dad—the tight jaw, tailored shoulders, sandy hair stiffly parted. Jon only looked at it once and put it away, but once he met Estelle, he shared it with her on a lazy evening as they sat in his apartment listening to the rain. Estelle glowed as if in love when she saw the photographs, the ads of Jon's father propped on a sleek car with a cigarette dangling from his fingers, or holding hands with a pretty girl as she twirled an umbrella on her shoulder. She glowed because the man in the photographs was so similar to the man sitting beside her and it gave her the notion she was on her way to spending her life with an undiscovered star.

She hasn't thought of the portfolio in a long time but she thinks of it now as she looks at Jon, his body stretched long, his face turned sideways on the pillow. She runs a finger along his temple, down his cheek, around his earlobe. He doesn't open his eyes and shifts and she leans down and kisses his ear, then she pulls the robe away from his neck and kisses the back of it. He shifts again and grunts and he has moved enough to where she can reach around and untie the robe.

He holds his breath, grunts again, his eyes shut tightly until she begins to kiss his stomach and he can only see Iris and he jerks and looks at her with his eyebrows raised in panic. Estelle says, "I didn't mean to scare you."

"I'm not scared," he says, and after a pause she leans over to kiss him and he pulls away.

"Not right now," he says, but he doesn't have to say anything, as the indifference is enough. She forgets the portfolio, forgets the rush that she barely recognized, and she gets up from the bed and walks into the living room.

"Estelle," he calls to her, but she doesn't answer. He gets dressed and asks if he can make dinner but she says she's not hungry. She stretches out on the couch under two blankets and changes the channels. For the rest of the night, he periodically asks if he can get her something to eat and she says no each time, until he gives up and is back in the bedroom watching the news. If a body has been found, he expects it to be a lead story. But there is nothing. To be certain, he watches through the weather and the soccer scores until the charming news crew signs off and promises to be back at seven in the morning. He gets up to check on Estelle and she is asleep, the remote nestled in her arms as if she loves it.

On Friday morning he fills the duffel bag and takes the poster tube and kisses Estelle good-bye. She gives her cheek and he hopes that by the evening she will have forgotten last night. Today is the last day of his free week and they have blanketed the city with the new photographs of Jennifer. Detective Marceau was in the habit of speaking with them at least once a week but he hasn't called in nine days. The weather has broken and the day is warm, the weekend looking even better, and the parks and streets will be filled with laughter and dogs and children. Jon takes off his coat as he walks back toward the metro. The cool morning air reminds him of walks with a young wife and a stroller, of kicking a ball with a little girl and the weight of the ball knocking her off balance, of playing hide-and-seek around the trunks of large trees and playground equipment. Of a green-eyed girl learning to read on a park bench, reciting colors and letters and looking up at her father to see if his head was nodding in approval. The small voice sounds in his head and he nods.

He comes to the metro but instead of going where he's supposed to go, he takes the train back to Abbesses. He walks to Iris's building and passes by. After several blocks, he comes to a church and a square courtyard is next to it, surrounded by a head-high, black iron fence with crosses on the top of each bar. A statue stands in the middle of the courtyard and the trees are bare but have the beginning of buds on their limbs. He opens the gate and follows a narrow gravel path to a concrete bench facing the statue. The sun shines on the face of the saint and the months of winter rain have streaked it gray. A book is tucked under the saint's arm and birds rest on his shoulders.

Jon wants to ask him about Jennifer but he knows what the saint

will say. He thinks about praying, but what for? Please forgive me
for screwing Iris and please bring my daughter home. He knows that
isn't the way it works and he can't convince himself to ask for help.
So he takes one more look at the saint and then he gets up, suddenly
uncomfortable surrounded by such defined lines of right and wrong.
He walks back into the street, and in another block, he sits down in a
café that is just opening and tries to put it together.

He orders coffee and before it is gone he has decided to go back and
see Iris. To ask again if she will paint his daughter. This time he will offer
more money. Or supplies. Whatever someone like her needs. There is a
jingle and a middle-aged couple walks in the doorway and sits at a table
next to him. The woman's right hand quivers and she holds it across the
table. She lets go momentarily and takes three bottles of pills from her
purse and sets them on the table. Then she holds his hand again.

Jon watches as the waitress brings them water and coffee, then the
woman gives her husband a handful of pills. He swallows one at a time,
smiling in between. When they are gone, she smiles back and says,
"Good."

He looks down at his coffee cup and wonders if he and Estelle will
ever be there.

One goddamn moment of peace. That's all I wanted, he thinks. A
moment he doesn't need now. He sees the star between her breasts
and he feels Estelle crawling into the bed and that moment of peace
has turned out to be a bad deal. But didn't he know it would be? That
somehow, it would end up in a bad deal. He wonders if coming clean
would be the best thing. Don't let it linger, go home and tell her. Estelle
understands many things, is patient, forgiving. But not that patient and
forgiving and how would he explain pulling Iris to the floor in search
of that glorious moment of peace that has no more luster. He watches
the couple and they don't speak, their eyes up and around the café
walls, out into the street, back and forth from each other. Content eyes.
Passive eyes. Eyes resting comfortably in a lazy morning, unimpeded
by the clutter of words. Jon shifts in his chair and his foot bumps the

duffel bag. Then he kicks it and the couple looks at him and his eyes aren't the same as theirs and they both turn away quickly.

He raises his hand and orders whiskey and the waitress laughs until she realizes he's not joking. He drinks and tries to decide between a friendship with Iris that might lead her to painting Jennifer, or breaking into her apartment and taking a few women for ransom until she agrees. This routine continues until late morning, and when he tries to get up and leave, the room spins and goes cloudy and he falls into an empty table. Other customers in for an early lunch look at him and cut their eyes at one another, shake their heads. The waitress helps him back into his chair and asks if he would like a glass of water. He brushes her off, mumbles something, gives her money. Then he picks up the bag and tube and makes for the door, his stride wobbly and the bag heavier than he remembered.

He weaves along the sidewalk, his throat burning and the glare of the sun forcing his eyes downward. Shoppers see him coming and move out of the way. At a tiny grocery he buys sunglasses and cigarettes, and when the cashier tells him to have a good day, he says, "Did you know that over thirty thousand people are reported missing in France every year?"

Out in the street he puts on the sunglasses and lights a cigarette, then unzips the duffel bag and pulls out a stack of pamphlets. "Look here! Win fifty thousand euros!" he says as he passes people walking along the sidewalk, getting off the bus, standing in the entrances of doorways. "Win fifty thousand euros! Make your dreams come true! Take that vacation you've always wanted to take! All you have to do is find the little girl!" Most step around, a few take the pamphlet. Two teenage boys follow behind him entertained, mocking the wobble in Jon's walk. He catches them in a store window and turns around. They back away but he holds out a pamphlet and says, "Here, here. No certain age required to be a winner." One of them punches the other in the shoulder and they turn and run away.

He starts along the sidewalk again, promoting the prize, shoving the pamphlet into purses and coat pockets of those who try to move around him. An old woman screams, "Police!" and then Jon screams back at her, "Yes! Police!" Soon he is giving the pamphlets away in handfuls, dropping them in mail slots, throwing them into the open doors of boutiques and restaurants. Voices threaten him but he ignores them and moves on, yelling, "Win fifty thousand euros!" and at the end of streets he takes lefts and rights without regard to direction until he has left a crooked trail of Jennifer's face through the once-quiet neighborhood. He stops twice to have another drink, proclaiming louder than before after each break. The lunchtime traffic comes and goes, and by the early afternoon, he runs out of pamphlets. He holds the duffel bag upside down and shakes it and one more falls out. Standing in the middle of the sidewalk, he holds the pamphlet above his head, then throws his head back, stretches out his arms, and yells toward the cloudless sky, "This one is for you! Fifty thousand big ones in the offering plate at Sunday mass if you would just set her on our goddamn doorstep!" Then he tears the pamphlet into pieces and tosses it into the air.

He lights another cigarette and keeps walking, quietly this time, until he finds a café. He sits at the bar and orders a beer, then he takes off the sunglasses. His head bobs forward and back and he nods off. The bartender sets the beer in front of him and claps his hands and Jon sits up straight. "You can't sleep in here," the bartender says. Jon stretches, makes fists and rubs his eyes. "What street is this?" he asks, and the bartender slides him a pack of matches. Le Café Perdu, 61 rue Abbesses. He looks around and a reddish-brown dog with a white nose lies at the end of the bar next to a bowl of water and a bowl of food. On the wall to the right of the bar, the woman leans against the rock, the waterfall behind her. Jon mumbles something and the bartender says, "Do you need a taxi?" He shakes his head and pays for the drinks and walks to Iris's apartment. She opens the door and he comes in without a word, lies down in the middle of the floor, his arms and legs spread wide like an X marking the spot.

6

Estelle takes the map from the wall and folds it, then she holds the handful of markers together and wraps a rubber band around them. She places it all in a shoe box and puts the shoe box on the top shelf of the hall closet. They have done all they can in one week and she has decided to put the plan away for the weekend. She ate lunch downstairs at M. Conrer's café and he urged her to get out and take a walk in the sunshine, and standing at the living room window, feeling the warmth on her face, she decides to take his advice. She puts on a sweater and leaves the jacket behind. When she walks past the café, she waves to M. Conrer through the window and he smiles back at her.

As she walks she remembers an afternoon like this, two, maybe three years ago, sitting on a blanket with Jon watching Jennifer play her first soccer match. The young girls moved in a pack around the ball, a shifting, awkward crowd that never moved very far in any direction. Parents cheered but mostly laughed and no one cared when the game ended without a score. Particularly Jennifer, who asked her father as they walked home, "Who won?"

It was during half time of the game, after Jennifer had run over and taken a drink of water from a squeeze bottle that she had declared necessary, that Estelle said to Jon, "She runs like you. With her knees nearly knocking together."

"Thank my father for that," he said. "Those fancy pictures make him look like a movie star but he had legs like a giraffe."

THE HANDS OF STRANGERS | 51

The game continued and Jon and Estelle snacked on sandwiches and Estelle occasionally called out to Jennifer, who would turn and wave, momentarily falling away from the pack, then she'd turn and run with wild knees and elbows to catch up. During a time-out close to the end of the game, Estelle lay back on the blanket, looked into the afternoon sky, and said, "You know, on days like this it feels like God has His finger right on top of your head, guiding you around like a stage puppet."

Jon looked at her, took a bite of sandwich, and said, "No more soccer games for you."

She reached up and tackled him down with her and said, "You understand what I mean. Don't you, Mr. Serious?"

"Yep."

"Yep? What is yep?"

"A lazy way of agreeing with you."

She took his hand and said, "Just look at the sky. It is empty. Only blue. It is nothing, but it is everything. I see everything in that sky."

A whistle blew and play continued and Jon said, "So you feel the finger of God on your head?"

"Yes. And not the pinkie, but the big finger. And it's on your head also whether you know it or not."

They heard the voices of parents and coaches shouting encouragement and they sat up and watched, neither of them speaking again until the game was over and Jennifer stood in front of them, asking if they could stop for pizza on the way home.

She remembers the day and she rubs the top of her head. She feels no finger. But the fresh air, the sunshine, escaping from the apartment—it gives her the idea that it may be close, hovering twenty or fifty or a hundred feet above her. Close. She stops at a magazine stand and buys a lottery card and sticks it in the back pocket of her jeans.

She has felt her faith renewed this week though no one has called and nothing has changed. Nothing but Jon. She has watched him leave the apartment each morning, the duffel bag filled, his shoulders drooping a little more today than the first of the week. She knows he tries to hide it but his eyes, his sighs, the monotone sound of his voice—it all suggests he is losing hope. Or has lost it. He is lying in the street, the taxi gone. She smells the liquor on his breath when he comes home, the mouthful of gum a sad defense. She wonders if her newfound optimism is enough for both of them. Or if he's the one that has it right.

She walks until she is close to the river. Detective Marceau has asked twice if they want it to be dragged and both times Estelle said no. He has convinced Estelle he is a good man—a father himself, a thin man with soft cheeks, a touch of empathy in his voice each time they speak. But she finds herself awake at night, wishing he were more like the men in the action movies, gruff and fearless and certain they will fix what is wrong.

She reaches the river and walks to the harbor. Long, expensive boats with their sails down sit close to one another, the water calm and the sun glaring across the clean white decks. Birds perch on masts and here and there men and women sit on deck at tables for two with bottles of wine and late lunches. She walks down the concrete stairs of the quay and along the row of boats. Despite the recent rain, the water has the stale smell of a shallow pond, and after admiring several of the larger boats, she climbs the stairs and sits on a bench that overlooks the harbor. She takes the lottery card from her pocket. Again she looks up for the finger.

It is early spring that always makes her think of the family flower shops, the doors wide open, the purples and yellows and reds, so true they looked fake. That smell of a thousand flowers that she would anticipate on her walk after school to the shop where her mother worked. Saying hi to everyone, asking for her father. Dropping her school bag in front of the cash register and her mother telling her to move it. If her father was there, at the end of the day he would let her spray the bouquets that sat in round black tubs on the sidewalk. Not too much, only give them a dew. Then later, as a young girl, running the cash register, making deliveries, finding streets she never knew existed. She looks across the harbor and hears her father's voice—keep the colors fresh, Madame So-and-So prefers the yellow lilies to the white and Monsieur What's-His-Name will be in twice a month for roses for the vases of his restaurant. Treat the bride-to-be as if she were inventing the idea of marriage. Don't let the employees smoke in the store. Pay the bills on time whether you have the money or not. Don't let your mother give away the store because she will, especially in the summer when the mothers walk in with their small children.

If she had the business now she wouldn't need the lottery ticket. But she let her parents sell and retire to the northern coast. Jon had come along, then Jennifer, and she didn't think running the business would be the same without her parents there. Jon told her she was making a mistake. She used to walk past the stores with Jennifer in a stroller, tell herself she hadn't.

She takes a coin from her pocket and reads the rules on the back of the card. Underneath the three circles are numbers one through nine. If all three numbers are the same, she is a big winner. If two are the same, she is just a winner. She flips the card and rubs the three silver circles. A four, a nine, a six. She folds the card and tosses it on the ground.

She gets up and walks away from the river, takes the long way home through neighborhoods that she hasn't seen in months. She notices a new bookstore, new paint on the face of an apartment building. She stops at an empty pizzeria and has a beer and a calzone. When she's done she heads toward home, content in the sunshine, her hands in her pockets and a rhythm in her walk and twice men stop and give her long, wolflike stares. The second time she winks at the man and he loses his nerve. She catches her reflection in a window and sees a younger Estelle, less aware. She looks around, up and down the street, at a sheet drying on a balcony, and in an instant it seems foreign to her, as if she has been picked up and put down in a city she has never seen before. She is a Parisian and has known nothing else, filled her entire life with an unspoken pride of knowing the sidewalks that don't find their names on the tourist maps. Unlike those who come for the spring, unlike those who put in a year or two and call it their own. The real thing. The real place. The swarms of wide-eyed visitors nothing more than part of her city, like a cloud of gnats hovering in her backyard. And now her city has displaced her, made her feel estranged, as if she woke one morning and the names of streets and cathedrals had been translated into a language she didn't speak. She looks back at her reflection and realizes that the city that once held her as its own now holds her at its mercy. She sits on the curb and smokes a cigarette, tosses pebbles at a pothole. Maybe Jon has it right, she thinks. Maybe the more pathetic and hopeless we become, the more likely the empathetic finger of God will attach itself to our heads.

After the cigarette, she walks home, less rhythm than before. At her building she avoids the elevator and walks up the stairs. She opens the door and expects to see Jon but he isn't home. She lies on the couch and kicks off her shoes. Her heartbeat slows and she feels the end creeping toward her. Creeping toward her from every corner of the room, seeping through the walls and ceiling, closing in on her like a slowly drifting fog. She closes her eyes and imagines the flowers, imagines the way she looked in her reflection. She tries to fight it off but it is unbeatable and she relents, lets her body absorb the unknown.

She opens her eyes and turns on the television. She takes the cigarettes from the coffee table and walks to the window and opens it. She lights the cigarette, looks down into the street. M. Conrer sweeps the sidewalk. An old woman watches her dog shit then she picks it up with a plastic bag. Estelle watches the street until she finishes the cigarette. She tosses the butt out of the window and goes into the kitchen. The cabinets are bare and she can't remember the last time they have been shopping the way that normal people shop. She closes the cabinet doors and looks at the telephone and the red message light blinks. She pushes the play button and a generic voice says, "You have two messages." Then she pushes the button again and hears the voice of Marceau.

Jon wakes and sits up and his temples throb. His neck is tight as he moves his head from side to side and he smacks his lips, his mouth dry and chalky. The tube and duffel bag are in the corner. The sun has fallen and a gray twilight fills the room like a fog. He goes into the kitchen and splashes water on his face and rinses his mouth, then he notices a note pinned to his shirt. He takes it off and reads, *Stay as long as you would like. Iris.* But he knows by the faded light that it is time to go.

He puts on his coat and picks up the bag and tube, but before he leaves he takes a quick stroll around the apartment. It is evident this is only where she works. He sees nothing but wine and water bottles in the kitchen—no refrigerator, no microwave. In another room are more portraits of the women and a pile of clean canvases. The bathroom is bare except for toilet paper, a bar of soap on the sink, and a clutter of dirty towels hanging on a rack. In the tub are recently rinsed brushes and the tub is splotchy with watered-down grays and oranges and greens. He reaches to open the door to another room down the small hallway from the bathroom but it is locked.

He walks back into the large room where the women sit on easels and he looks them over. None have the draw of the woman on the café wall. So he reaches for the one nearest—the half-dressed woman sitting on the concrete steps of a vague building—and he rolls her up and puts her in the tube with Jennifer. As he leaves and walks into the street, he looks both ways for Iris, wonders where she eats her meals, bathes, falls asleep.

His headache is sharp and he stops for aspirin at a magazine stand before he goes down to the metro. The man behind the counter looks at him and laughs, says something in an Eastern language to the woman unpacking a box of postcards. She looks at Jon and cuts her eyes back at the man and throws her hands up in celebration and they laugh together. Jon pays for the aspirin and walks down the street, feels the eyes of the neighborhood on him. The morning comes back to him in a cloud. The proclamations, the reaching for strangers. He sees the sign for the metro at the end of the street and he hurries, walks with his head down, eager to disappear below, where no one looks anywhere but straight ahead.

~

He opens the apartment door and Estelle rushes over to him before he can get the door closed.

"Listen, listen," she says, almost breathless. She grabs his arm and pulls him into the kitchen. "Listen to the message. Marceau." She pushes play and then she clenches her fists and holds them under her chin.

"What is it?" he asks and she puts her hand over his mouth.

After a beep, the recorded Detective Marceau says, "Estelle and Jon, this is Detective Marceau and I would like to talk with you as soon as you receive this message. We have some information regarding Jennifer. It is only information but it is helpful so telephone me when you hear this."

The message ends, and there is another beep, and it is Marceau again with the same message.

"Twice," she says. "It must be something important. He has never called twice."

"You haven't called yet?"

"I was waiting for you."

"Don't wait," Jon says. "Call. Now, now, now."

Estelle takes the phone and they sit on the edge of the couch. Jon's right leg bounces. Estelle misdials once and starts over. Marceau answers on the third ring and she says, "Detective Marceau, this is Estelle and we have the two messages. What is it?"

"Estelle, yes. Is Jon with you?"

"Right here."

He clears his throat and says, "Wait for a moment, please."

"What is it?" Jon says.

"I'm on hold."

Jon leans forward, rubs his hands together, the pain in his head and neck forgotten. Estelle's eyes are wide and tentative. Marceau returns and says, "Sorry, I wanted to get the information correct before we spoke. Please understand this is nothing absolute but it is more than we have had."

"Just say it," Estelle says. Jon puts his head next to hers to share the receiver.

"This morning we received a phone call from an unidentified woman who says she saw a young girl at the RER station at Les Saules who fit Jennifer's description. Her hair was cut short and she was wearing boy's clothes but the woman believes it was the same child she has seen in your poster. She was with two middle-aged men. According to the woman, she tried to speak to the girl but the men took her by the arms and left the station quickly."

"She didn't follow them?"

"Unfortunately, no. But she gave us a description of the men and we have had officers in the area all afternoon. We will keep an alert in the area for some time. This is not great news, but it is news. At the least, it gives hope that she is alive."

Estelle gives the phone to Jon and covers her mouth with her hand and begins to cry.

"Hello?" Marceau says.

"That's good," Jon says. "Is there anything we can do?"

"Not now. I will call you again soon."

Jon hangs up and sets the phone on the coffee table. Estelle falls across his lap and he leans on her. After several minutes she stops crying and they sit up. Look at each other. Don't say anything. They sit close together on the couch until the last remnants of daylight fade and the apartment grows dark except for the light in the kitchen. Jon begins to speak once but stops himself. The street traffic disappears as the evening transforms into night and only an occasional passing car breaks the silence. Estelle pushes Jon to the end of the couch and lays a pillow in his lap, then she stretches out. She turns on her side and in minutes she falls asleep. He slumps, lays back his head, and stares at the dark ceiling. He imagines the faces of the middle-aged men who are handling his daughter—thin, sunken faces, strange bloodshot eyes and contorted smiles, the same face divided by two, twice the ugliness. The faces float around the ceiling and then there aren't only faces, but four arms, four hands, holding her and cutting her fine, brown hair, putting her into clothes that don't fit. Two voices daring her to speak once outside the door.

At least, it gives us hope that she is alive, he hears Marceau say. He looks down at Estelle. Her mouth is open and her breaths long and he brushes a strand of hair away from the corner of her mouth and remembers the day they met on the train. The way he brushed her hair away and she opened her eyes and said thank you. The way the world opened up in front of him at that moment, this city, this life, racing toward him with the speed of the train. And now this woman in his lap in this city that was once an open-ended question but now shrinking, disappearing a little more each week, its answer to the direct question the same day after day, a bland, apathetic no. But today its answer is maybe. His leg has fallen asleep but he doesn't move. He can almost hear footsteps in the hallway, the small voice asking if it can stay up longer. He closes his eyes and this time there is another face with the two men, the face of Iris, wide-eyed and alive. He squeezes his eyes tighter but it won't go away, moves in front of the other two, opens its mouth to speak, but he opens his eyes and shakes his head and chases it away. Estelle moves, makes a short, childlike snore. He puts his hand on her hip, then rubs his fingertips along her leg, up her arm, across the back of her neck, hoping that there is a way back.

7

Jon falls asleep with Estelle in his lap and they don't move for several hours. Estelle wakes a little past midnight, sits up and rubs her eyes, then she walks to the window. The night is deep and the streets are quiet. Jon feels her move and wakes and she tells him to stretch out on the couch, that she is up for a while.

She walks into the hallway toward their bedroom, but as she passes Jennifer's half-open door she pauses, then gently pushes the door open. She takes two slow, careful steps into the room and stops, looks around, breathes in with hopes of smelling her smell. The shades in the room are down and the light from the street is blocked out and the room is dark like a closet. She walks over and sits on the bed and turns on the lamp of the bedside table.

With the light come the colors—the pink sheets, the white comforter, the rainbow rug at the foot of the bed, the yellows and blues from the open closet. Estelle takes the bed pillow and holds it close to her chest, then she rocks and hums. She breathes in again but the smell is gone and she squeezes the pillow tighter, then she lies down on the bed, the pillow wrapped under her.

It is the first time she has lain in Jennifer's bed. She has been afraid to spend too much time in the room, afraid that being in her place might be a sign of replacing her, of moving on. But as she lies in the bed now, the fit of her body to the twin-size bed pacifies her, holds her like a hand holding a wounded bird. She rolls on her back and looks at the ceiling and wonders what Jennifer imagines at night when she looks at the same ceiling but her thoughts drift and she can't find herself in Jennifer's head. She tries to remember what she imagined as a little girl and it too is absent and she wonders what good it is anyway. If you can't remember what you once imagined, what is the point in imagining? What is real is what is strong and she touches her finger to her nose and presses until it hurts. Then she pinches the back of her arm until she loses her breath. Then she pulls her eyebrow until several hairs pop out and she looks at them on her fingertip. What is real is what is strong. She blows the eyebrow hair from her fingertip, takes the pillow from her chest, and puts it behind her head.

"God?" she says aloud.

The quiet in the apartment is stale and almost smells.

"God?" she says again, and a car horn sounds. She reaches over and turns off the lamp. I can see better like this, she thinks, and there is Jennifer moving around the room, going through drawers and changing clothes until she is satisfied.

As a child Estelle prayed because she was told, as a teenager she prayed because she was trained, as a young woman she prayed when she remembered, and as an adult she prayed when she felt a need. As the mother of an abducted child she prayed because she didn't know what else to do. She asked Jon once if he had been praying and he said, "I'll do whatever you want me to do."

"We're dangling at the end of a rope," she said. "You know that, don't you?"

"A drowning man will grasp for straws."

"What?"

"Nothing. Just something an old basketball coach used to say."

"What's it mean?"

"I don't know. He used to say something about horseshoes and hand grenades and making love too. He used to say a lot of dumb shit."

"What does that have to do with praying?"

"I don't think anything."

She stares at him and sometimes she wants to choke him. But not now. Not after the news. The only news. She sits up in the bed and watches Jennifer put on a sweater she has outgrown, tight through her shoulders and an inch from her wrists. She takes it off and holds it up, looks at it as if the sweater didn't understand it was to grow with her. Then she tosses it in the corner and puts her hands on her hips, wondering what to do next. She moves to the closet and gets on her knees and picks through the shoes. She makes two piles in the floor, one for the shoes she likes and one for the shoes she doesn't like. When she is done she puts the shoes she likes back into the closet and slides the dislikes under the bed. She moves to the toy box next, but before she can open it, there is a rumble of thunder that distracts Estelle and Jennifer fades.

Estelle stands and walks into the living room. Jon sleeps soundly and she notices he hasn't taken off his shoes. She carefully unties and slides them off and he doesn't move. Then she takes the cigarettes and an ashtray from the coffee table and a bottle of water from the refrigerator and goes back into Jennifer's room. She sits in the middle of the floor and lights a cigarette. "Yeah, I can see better like this," she whispers, and the child begins to move again.

Beautiful dreams full of numbers. A crowd on a boardwalk watching fireworks. An army of coyotes playing tug-of-war with a bone as long as a flagpole. In another, he has a big family, eight brothers and sisters, and they're all there, laughing and arguing and slapping one another in the arm. But they don't have names, and when Jon asks them, they laugh big, will say anything to keep from giving him names. He doesn't know whose house they are in but it's old, and when he looks out of the window there's no street or neighborhood or city lights, only a flat field that runs into a dull horizon. He shifts from happy to frustrated, knows that these people share his blood but they won't be handled too carefully. But even frustrated, it's a room of people all pieces of him, all familiar with one another. One by one they leave until he's alone and then he notices there's no furniture in the room and the window is shrinking. The room gets smaller and smaller until he opens the door and walks out and there's a forest where the open field used to be and it's so dark. He walks into the woods and the only sound is the crunch of leaves under his feet. No birds, no squirrels, no snakes. He stops and leans on a tree and the tree is rotted and falls over, then he moves to another tree and gives it a shove and the same thing. And another, and they start to fall like dominoes and he turns to run back toward the house, leaping and ducking, but he's lost and only running and running, dodging crashing trees and looking into the sky for some light to steer him but in every direction the sky is mud.

Jon wakes with a jerk, sits up, then falls back again. Estelle calls out to him from Jennifer's room and he says he's okay.

"What are you doing in there?" he asks.

Estelle leaves the child's bedroom, walks into the living room, and turns on a lamp. Jon shields his eyes, then rolls over and puts his face into the sofa pillow. Estelle sits on the floor.

"It feels different tonight, doesn't it?"

Jon answers into the pillow and it comes out in a mumble.

"What did you say?"

He turns to her and says, "He said don't get excited." In her face he sees that he's too late, that she's decided this is it. In only a few hours, a lift has appeared in her tired eyes.

"Her smell is gone," she says.

Jon sits up on the couch, stretches his arms and twists, then says, "I went in there last week and noticed the same thing."

"Do you think it's her?"

"I don't know. He said don't get excited."

"You already said that."

Jon stands and goes into the kitchen and makes coffee. The microwave clock reads 3:59, the first morning light of a hopeful day still hours away. Jon brings over coffee for both of them and Estelle turns on the television. They drink the coffee and watch the television screen with blank stares, too aware that nothing is on at four in the morning. Estelle flips through the channels for half an hour until she tosses the remote to Jon and says, "I need a bath."

Estelle goes into the bathroom and runs a bath and lights a handful of candles. Jon listens until the water stops and Estelle splashes into the tub, then he goes into the kitchen and washes his face with cold water.

~

They spend Saturday processing the good news, trying to stay even, discussing what they should do. The day drags as a nervous energy fills the apartment that no chore or meal or movie can pacify. "Tomorrow," Jon says around midnight, "we have to get out of here." Sunday morning they are up early, and after quick showers and a quick breakfast, Estelle and Jon ride the RER to Les Saules. The plan is to walk and look.

The neighborhood is what Jon has imagined in a place where children are hidden. Despite the crisp morning, the air is strange, somewhat thick and humid, as if they got off the RER in another country instead of another part of the city. The faces of the buildings are worn and colorless. On street corners, men huddle in small clusters around square tables filled with watches or fake leather or cartons of cigarettes. Jon and Estelle pass the tables without paying much attention, but that doesn't deter the random peddler who will walk along with them for seven or eight steps and offer gold necklaces or Eiffel Tower key chains. Some of the men are old, some young, but all share the same expression—if you need it I got it. Jon exchanges looks with them hoping he will recognize the man who has taken his daughter by a particular eye color or scar, but they mistake his stare as interest and he has to tell them no several times, even has to push a more ambitious peddler away as he tries to wrap a silver bracelet around Estelle's wrist as she walks.

The morning seems to belong to the peddlers as the shops are closed on Sunday, and no one else is on the street, as if the buildings were only a movie set of a long-forgotten production. Estelle holds Jon's arm, and after they have walked for ten minutes, the street peddlers thin out and they slow their pace. Estelle asks Jon what to look for and he can't find a way to answer. Rusty iron gates are pulled across the front of stores and restaurants and Jon stops once to peek inside a closed café, though he doesn't know why. They weave through the streets without direction, and as the morning grows on, the sunshine breaks through a thin film of clouds and more women and children appear, though they look at Estelle and Jon much like the men did, as if they are waiting for the opportune moment to take what they want.

There is graffiti along the bases of most of the buildings, like a belt wrapped around the city blocks, the greens and blues and reds faded by the sun and the rain. The graffiti reaches as high as the artist could reach. Jon and Estelle pass from street to street, surrounded by large, loopy letters that spell unreadable words, cartoonish cats and dogs, sensationalized faces with open mouths and bulging eyes, topless women. Each street is the same as the one before. And a smell lingers around every corner. The smell of a place that has quit trying. At a street corner, they stop and look around and Jon feels in his coat for cigarettes but has forgotten them at home.

"This place is hollow," Estelle says. "Everything. Everyone. I wish we wouldn't have come."

Jon says, "I can see why the woman who called the police didn't follow."

"Have you noticed anyone that might be one of Marceau's men?"

"No. Have you?"

"Maybe. I don't know. Do you think they know who we are?"

"Who?"

"The people around here. The men trying to sell us stuff."

"I doubt it. Why should they?"

"I don't know," she says again. "Are we sure this is the place Marceau said?"

"This is it."

Again they look up and down the street and neither remembers the direction of the train station. Jon begins to offer a direction, but Estelle turns to him and says, "Do you feel her?"

Jon sighs, pauses. Then says, "I want to."

"I thought we would. I didn't expect this."

"Neither did I."

"Maybe she can feel us," Estelle says. "Maybe she's behind one of these walls and when we walked by she could feel us."

"Or maybe she's not around here anymore," Jon says. "And that's why we can't feel her."

Estelle shakes her head, looks as if she wants to try and answer, but can't make sense of the words. Instead of speaking, she leans her face into Jon's chest and he hugs her.

"Do you want to go home?"

She nods. Then she wraps her arms around his waist and they sway together. In the distance a police siren sounds and they hear a rush of shouts, sharp and clean like barking dogs, from a couple of blocks away.

"Okay," he says. "Let's go. But let's promise to forget about today. About this place. Don't talk about it. Nothing."

Estelle steps back and says, "Yes. Let's promise. Keep thinking about the good news."

"The good news. We never came here."

"Never," she answers, and she takes one more look around. "Never."

She grabs Jon's hand and they begin to search for a train station stop or a taxi. The sirens draw closer. The shouts of a few become the shouts of many and they seem to amplify along the bare streets. Estelle holds Jon's hand more tightly and they walk faster than they did before, until the shouts shrink away and they feel as if they have escaped from somewhere.

8

On Monday Jon returns to work at L'École des Langues, and when he comes out of the building at five o'clock, he finds Marceau waiting on the sidewalk. Marceau walks over to him and offers a cigarette, then says, "Can I walk with you for a moment?"

Jon nods and reaches for the cigarette and knocks it to the ground. Marceau picks it up and says, "A long day?"

Jon nods again, and says, "Which way?"

"No matter." Marceau wears a hat and gloves though the bite of winter is gone except for the early mornings. They smoke and walk and Jon asks if he has news.

"No. Not today. But soon, we hope. I have something else to ask you."

Jon puts the cigarette to his mouth and notices his fingers shaking and he drops the cigarette again. He steps on it as if he were done and says, "Sure. What is it?"

Marceau reaches into the pocket of his overcoat and pulls out one of the new pamphlets of Jennifer. He holds the pamphlet toward Jon and they stop, and Marceau says, "This is nice work. Very clear, very good photo. Thorough information. And now we have a lead because you and Estelle have done so much to help. But I have heard complaints about the man who was giving them away a few days ago at Abbesses. Do you know something about this?"

Jon rubs his forehead, then he says, "I was having a bad day."

Marceau takes Jon by the arm and they walk again. Marceau says, "I understand that you are having bad days. But you cannot run around the city drunk, screaming, and scaring old women who are walking down the street. From what I hear, people were very patient with you. If you expect to get this done in the right way, then you are going to have to control yourself during these bad days. No more throwing these things into the doorways of restaurants or open doors of buses. If you make this a joke, that is how people will take it. And I know you don't want this to be taken as a joke. Do you?"

They reach the corner and stop for the light to change. Jon says, "I will do better. That hasn't been a habit."

"I know. That's why we are talking now. So it won't be. If you need to drink and scream, go out of town. Or do it at home. When Estelle is not there."

Jon nods and says, "Do me a favor and don't mention this to her."

"I'm not. I think this is something we can keep to ourselves."

The light changes and the crowd crosses the street. Marceau shakes Jon's hand and says he will call, then he turns around and walks back toward Jon's office. Jon watches until Marceau makes a turn and is out of sight. He feels sweat under his arms and he takes off his coat and folds it over his arm. The light changes and he waits with others on the corner until it is time to walk again, then he crosses the street to the metro and goes home. The days are slowly growing longer and the last light of day remains as he walks along his street, the sidewalks busy with bodies ready for home. He comes to M. Conrer's café and on the sidewalk are a handful of small, round tables for two that weren't there when Jon walked by on his way to work in the morning. The same tables have appeared in front of cafés and restaurants all over the city in recent days, as if they had been lying dormant under the sidewalks all winter, staying warm, shielded away from the cold rain, and now eager to sprout through the cracks with the first days of sunshine. M. Conrer's tables are in a clutter, without chairs, and a boy wearing an apron comes out and wipes the tops and legs with a damp rag. Jon stops and watches him and finishes a cigarette. The boy asks Jon if he wants a whiskey but Jon says he'll come inside for it.

Jon walks in and over to a bar stool. The café is empty except for an old woman reading the newspaper. Dirty plates and glasses fill several of the tables as if a crowd has just left. M. Conrer appears from the kitchen door, sees Jon, and he claps his hands and smiles and says, "Yes. Yes. The good news has arrived. I told you that you were closer. Didn't I? Didn't I say that you were closer?"

The old man reaches over the bar and shakes Jon's hand violently and his grin is full, almost stupid. Jon knows Estelle has been here for lunch and only God knows what promises she and M. Conrer have made each other about Jennifer. Twenty-four hours? Within the week? At least this month? He gets his hand away from M. Conrer and the man is so enthusiastic, he wonders if Jennifer isn't waiting in the kitchen as a surprise.

"Didn't I say that?" M. Conrer keeps repeating until Jon nods and smiles to shut him up. All I want is a drink, he wants to say. But instead he says, "You said it. You were right."

"Every moment you are closer."

"Every moment."

And then there is silence, only more nodding and smiling, as if the optimism needed its own space to soak in. Jon looks over at the old woman and she turns the pages of the newspaper. He looks back at M. Conrer and his expression hasn't changed and Jon says, "I bet you have some whiskey back there."

"Oh. Yes, yes," he answers, and he sets a glass on the bar and pours. "Such a busy day. Estelle with the news and time to put the tables out and so many for lunch that we run out of the special and these tables still filled with plates. All day a race. This time of year seems filled with miracles. It is your time."

"If you say so."

"It is. Estelle believes it. You can see by the color of her face that she believes it. There is blood in her cheeks again."

"We haven't been made any promises."

"No. Not yet. But it's a sign. Like the first warm sun."

Someone calls from behind the swinging door and M. Conrer says he'll be back and he goes into the kitchen. Jon drinks slowly and takes in small bits of the old man's enthusiasm. Today he can understand it, can feel closer to it. He looks at himself in the bar mirror and checks for blood in his own cheeks but his face is the same pale face he has looked at all winter.

M. Conrer returns and says, "Why don't you call Estelle and ask her to come down? Have some wine and I will make you a good meal." Jon nods and M. Conrer hands him the phone from behind the bar. Estelle agrees, and after Jon hangs up the phone, he moves to the only clean, empty table. M. Conrer calls to the boy wiping the tables outside, and when he comes inside, he and M. Conrer bus the dirty tables, M. Conrer directing in quick snaps—take this, empty this, hold this, come back for this. Once the tables are clear, the boy takes the rag and wipes away the crumbs and spills and then he begins to sweep. M. Conrer brings over a carafe of wine and sits down with Jon. He's short of breath and he wipes his moist brow with the back of his hand. "I'm getting old," he says, then he notices that he forgot glasses and he's up again. Jon watches the woman finish the newspaper, then fold it neatly and stick it in her purse. Jon has never seen her before but she mentions to M. Conrer that she will see him tomorrow and M. Conrer answers with, "The usual." Then she puts on her coat and hooks the purse over her shoulder and she walks out, looks into the sky, and shakes her head as if she disagrees with the order of the clouds. Estelle appears and bumps into the woman as she walks with her eyes still toward the sky. The purse falls from her shoulder and they both apologize as Estelle bends to pick it up.

Jon smiles as he watches Estelle stoop for the purse. She wears her black sweater that fits snugly around her waist and hips and reaches her knees. When she bends the sweater drags the ground and hides her legs and her body disappears behind the black. Estelle puts the newspaper back into the purse and stands, and when she does it's like a lift-off, the sweater falling open and her innocent smile and trim figure an awakening to Jon and he catches himself on the verge of crying. He puts his fist to his mouth and presses, bends his head and closes his eyes until the threat of tears subsides, and he looks up again and the woman and Estelle are talking, the woman's arm around Estelle's waist. The old woman has a consoling air as she speaks and Estelle listens. He sees the color in her cheeks that M. Conrer noticed, the renewed, rosy blood. The woman stops talking and she and Estelle hug and again Jon fights off the need to lay his head on the table and sob in heavy heaves, without a care for where he is or who is watching. Estelle turns to walk in the door and she sees herself in the window's reflection and she brushes her hair away from her face, straightens her sweater, adjusts her belt buckle over the button of her jeans. Once she's satisfied, she opens the door and she waves to Jon, who can only smile, then look away, afraid that anything else from her will cause him to let it go.

"Estelle," M. Conrer calls out, and he comes over and kisses her. This gives Jon time to take a deep breath and gather himself, then he stands and greets Estelle in the same way, except that after he kisses her, he puts his arms around her waist and hugs until she makes a little grunt. "You're killing me," she says and he lets go and kisses her again on the cheek.

They sit and M. Conrer brings wineglasses to the table and tells them to relax, sit back, and talk to each other. He asks if they want a salad and Estelle does and Jon doesn't. He fills their glasses from the carafe then goes toward the kitchen, looking over his shoulder at them before he pushes through the swinging door.

Estelle folds her arms on the table. Jon slumps in his chair. They both look out of the window and back at each other.

"How was today?" she asks.

He shrugs and says, "A day." Then he reaches for his glass, bumps it, and several drops of red spill on the table. Estelle slips her hand into the cuff of her sweater and starts to wipe away the wine. "Don't," Jon says and he grabs her wrist. "I like that sweater."

"It has wiped up more than this," she answers. And it has. Ketchup from Jennifer's mouth, dripping ice cream from Jennifer's hand, blood from Jennifer's knee. "Isn't there a saying about old habits?" she asks, and then she forces a smile. He lets go of her wrist and she wipes the wine.

"You look nice," Jon says.

"Two compliments already? Is there something you want?"

"Only what Conrer said. To sit and relax and talk and have a good meal with good wine."

"With me?"

"With you."

Estelle reaches across the table and lays her hands out with the palms up. Jon sits straight and puts his hands in hers. Her hands are warmer than they have been. She wears eyeliner and earrings and perfume.

"I feel like something will happen," she says.

"Something already has."

She squeezes his hand when he answers. A positive word, she thinks. Finally, a positive word. She wonders if he has noticed the small extras of her appearance. She wants to say that she has also painted her toenails, shaved her legs, pretended that today was a normal day. But she doesn't wonder long as he continues to look at her like she is the woman he loves. M. Conrer walks in from the kitchen with Estelle's salad, but when he sees them holding on to each other across the table, he slips back through the door unnoticed.

No other voices. No clanging from the kitchen. For the moment, no one passes along the sidewalk. One moment of peace, Jon thinks as he looks at her. And it is here, in this pause.

"Do you think Monsieur Conrer would notice if we left?" Estelle asks.

"He may notice but he wouldn't care. Do you want to go upstairs?"

"No. Anywhere but upstairs."

"Okay."

They stand and walk out of the café. Several blocks away, along the walk to the metro, is a one-star hotel stuck between a wine store and butcher shop. Jon and Estelle walk in that direction without a word. They arrive and a frumpy middle-aged woman sits at a desk folding pillowcases. Jon asks for a room and she looks at them curiously when she notices they are without luggage. She looks Estelle up and down and Estelle winks at her. The woman takes a key from the wall and they follow her up a skinny staircase to the second floor. Jon takes the key and says thanks and the woman is slow to leave, as if waiting on them to explain. Jon says thanks again and Estelle wants to shove her along but she finally turns and goes down the stairs. The room is musty and square and Jon opens the window and Estelle moves behind him and pulls his shirt out of his pants. The evening is still as Parisian families are settling into dinner, as stores are closing, as the night falls and hides away the dirt. Jon and Estelle reach for each other slowly, cautiously, protecting themselves from any quick, abrupt shift that might shatter a moment's fragility.

⬤

"It's the first miracle," Estelle had said to M. Conrer that morning as she sat at the bar and drank her coffee. He nodded his approval, squeezed her hands, sat with her at the bar while the boy made espressos and served bread to the regular morning traffic. It was M. Conrer who had suggested to her weeks ago that finding Jennifer would be a series of small miracles, a trail of the unexplained that would come in small bits, forming the whole, not the grand spectacle of the movies. "You have to see the little signs, the little miracles that will happen along the way," he had told her. "Don't wait on the big dose." And she believed that Detective Marceau's message was the beginning. At least there is hope she is alive. A woman saw her and called to her and she turned her head to answer but was hurried away by those who have claimed her. It was real. It came from the mouth of the police. It happened and it would happen again. M. Conrer felt a sense of pride as he watched Estelle revel in the belief that a miracle had occurred.

She sat in the café through the morning and then she ate an early lunch and went upstairs. The first miracle, she repeated to herself as she picked up around the apartment, washed a load of clothes, cleaned out the refrigerator. She liked the way it sounded as it moved from her throat into the silence. The r's gave it a solid foundation, the five syllables gave it a rhythm. *The* made it official. The first miracle.

Once the chores were finished, she sat on the sofa, propped her feet on the coffee table, and smoked a cigarette. Jon wouldn't be home for several more hours and she wasn't sure if she should let her enthusiasm run its course before he arrived or if she should hold it over, force-feed it to him, make him see it her way. Repeating the phrase again, she became certain that she had seen things his way long enough. "Here, Jon," she would say. "Open up. Wider than that. Wider. Now take this. Swallow it. It'll make you feel better, I promise. No, no, don't close your mouth. Chew it. Chew it up and swallow. It's for your own good." She put out her cigarette and laughed sarcastically. He wasn't that easy. She had already tried M. Conrer's theory of small miracles on him one evening over dinner and Jon had said, "I didn't know miracles came in degrees." She didn't argue. The next evening she brought it up again and he said, "Well, if they're so small, aren't they coincidences instead of miracles? Like when two people who don't know each other find out they both know somebody else. Ask Conrer that. I bet he sees it as a miracle if he finds an umbrella on a rainy day. When there's a miracle, we'll know it. We won't have to look for it."

The following morning she asked M. Conrer Jon's question. And that's when he said, "Jon is waiting on a crash of lightning or a chariot arriving from the sky with Jennifer holding the reins. It is hard to hope when you wait on that kind of answer. That places a large wall between yes and no. Too tall to get over on a regular day."

M. Conrer's answer was enough for Estelle and from then on she waited. Waited, with her eyes open and alert, for the first domino to fall. And as far as she was concerned, it had. If Jon didn't want to accept it, no matter. For the moment, she believed.

She got up from the couch and walked to the bookcase in the corner of the room and looked for the Bible. She had found it on the shelf nearest the floor, tucked between a cookbook and a travel guide. The Bible belonged to her and it was black with gold leafing and a bookmark was placed in Psalms. She again sat on the sofa and opened it and it was stiff and noisy. She turned to the bookmark and she didn't recognize a passage and she wondered why the bookmark had been placed there.

She knew the Bible was filled with miracles but she didn't know where to find any, so she turned to the index in the back and ran her finger past the *K*s and *L*s until she arrived at *Miracles*. Under *Miracles* was a list of passages half a page long. The Gospels held the most references and she chose the book of Matthew. The first reference led her to chapter eight. Her Bible used headers to separate the topics of each passage, and the heading of chapter eight was *The Man with Leprosy*: "A man with leprosy came and knelt before him and said, 'Lord, if you are willing, make me clean.' Jesus reached out his hand and touched the man. 'I am willing,' he said. 'Be clean.' Immediately he was cured of his leprosy."

Is that it? she thought. No crowds? No applause? No oohs and aahs?

Chapter nine, *Jesus Heals a Paralytic*: "Some men brought to him a paralytic, lying on a mat. When Jesus saw their faith, he said to the paralytic, 'Take heart, son; your sins are forgiven.'" Again, Estelle wondered if that was all there was to it? She kept reading, and several verses later, Jesus tells the paralytic to get up, take your mat, and go home. And the man got up and went home.

She continued through chapter nine to *A Dead Girl and a Sick Woman*: "A ruler came and knelt before him and said, 'My daughter has just died. But come and put your hand on her, and she will live.' Jesus got up and went with him, and so did his disciples. Just then a woman who had been subject to bleeding for twelve years came up behind him and touched the edge of his cloak. She said to herself, 'If I only touch his cloak, I will be healed.' Jesus turned and saw her. 'Take heart, daughter,' he said, 'your faith has healed you.' And the woman was healed from that moment. When Jesus entered the ruler's house and saw the flute players and the noisy crowd, he said, 'Go away. The girl is not dead, but asleep.' But they laughed at him. After the crowd had been put outside, he went in and took the girl by the hand, and she got up."

She continued to read about the blind and the mute, about the healing of two demon-possessed men, about the fever of Peter's mother-in-law. The sentences sounded the same in each of the miracles. Do you have faith? Yes. Then you are healed.

The passages were concise. The action fundamental. The result a reward. There was no prestory, no explanation of how those who were healed came to need healing in the first place. Only that He walked among them and rewarded their faith. It seemed too basic. But that was what M. Conrer had said. Look for the miracles in the everyday, in the basics. Don't wait on the crash of lightning. There hadn't been with Him, so why should there be now? That's what she would tell Jon.

Estelle spent the rest of the afternoon reading and rereading the miracles. She moved from Matthew to Mark to Luke, the authors different but the language the same. Once she was finished, she closed the Bible and returned it to the shelf, then she stretched and walked over to the window and opened it. She looked down at the tops of passing heads. Fewer hats every day. Longer light every day. She noticed the tables on the sidewalk of M. Conrer's café and the boy wiping them. Jon would be home any minute. She closed the window and leaned her head against it.

Do you have faith? she thought. Yes. Then . . .

Much left to be answered. Keep trying. But for her, the first miracle had occurred. She moved away from the window, went to the kitchen, and peeled an orange. As she sat on the sofa eating the orange slices, Jon called from downstairs and asked her to come and have dinner, that M. Conrer wouldn't let him take no for an answer. She got up, changed her clothes, went to the bathroom and brushed her hair, cleaned and fixed her face, all the while looking at herself in the mirror with uncertainty, unsure if it was okay to feel optimistic about what was to come.

And now, in the middle of the night, she gets out of bed, covers her naked body with the black sweater, and goes to the glass door that opens onto the small balcony of the hotel room. She pauses and looks at Jon, asleep on his back, and she believes she has seen the second miracle in the look on his face in the café. The lack of cynicism when she offered hope, the simplicity with which he sat with her, and talked with her, and walked with her, and made love with her. She hadn't said a word about her afternoon with the New Testament books. She hadn't used one of the bits of ammunition she had prepared to bring him to her side. All she had done was walk down to the café and he was changed. All the way? Probably not. Some? Yes. Increments, she thinks. Small, small steps to the end.

She walks onto the balcony. Four blocks to her left is their apartment. She feels the same breeze, looks at the same lights across the same city. The same quiet of the deep Paris night surrounds her. She has sat with it over and over, hour after hour, looking into the dark, wondering. She takes a long breath as an empty taxi turns onto the street and passes underneath her. The wind is cool and slides up her leg and she wraps her sweater tightly and folds her arms. Jon coughs in his sleep, then tosses and turns for a moment before settling, but she ignores him, doesn't take her eyes away from the dark that will soon again be light.

9

She has the windows open for the first time of the season and a bluebird sits on the window ledge. Iris dabs the brush onto the canvas, then tilts her head, steps back, and analyzes the part in Jennifer's hair. The apartment door is also open and an easy breeze makes its way from room to room. She has been working on the portrait for a week straight, taking no breaks to work on the other women, typically with both the apartment and bedroom doors locked, but this afternoon is too clear, too new to keep closed up. It has been a couple of weeks since she has seen Jon. She doesn't expect him and she works comfortably in the spring air, unafraid of being found out.

She has made changes to Jennifer's image. The child's hair is pulled back in a ponytail in the poster photograph, but Iris has let it down and it reaches Jennifer's thin shoulders. In the poster photograph, the background is nondescript, but Iris has placed Jennifer in the beginnings of a classroom. Over her left shoulder is a bookshelf not yet filled with books. Over her right shoulder is what appears to be a teacher's desk, littered with papers to grade, a coffee cup filled with pencils, and a pair of eyeglasses. Iris has also bared the child's neck, which is covered in the photograph with a turtleneck sweater. For Iris, Jennifer wears a tank top, and her neck is long and pale and unblemished.

She goes into the bathroom and washes the brush, then she shoos the bird off the ledge and closes the window. She leaves the apartment without locking the door and walks to a sandwich stand. She takes a ham and cheese sandwich and a Coke and she walks until she comes to a quaint, square playground, budding trees standing at each corner of the surrounding fence. Wood chips cover the ground and a bicycle with its front tire missing lies next to a seesaw. The playground is empty in the midday and Iris sits down at the base of a silver slide and unwraps the sandwich.

The playground is where she watches. Every week, she comes to the playground and stands on the sidewalk, with her arms propped on the waist-high wooden gate, and watches the women who watch their children. Their one eye always just over the top of the magazine. Their hand dangling over the crossed legs. Their cigarette burning to a nub. Their short, sure commands that make children change directions. She has watched the women and taken them with her back to the apartment, where they fill her days and nights. Where she gives them something other than children and wedding rings as she lets them question from behind the black faces. They do question, don't they? she has asked herself. Or do playgrounds and sack lunches answer their questions? Is it as simple as they make it seem as they wipe noses and kiss bumped heads and hand out cookies?

She breaks off a piece of bread and tosses it toward a pigeon poking around in the wood chips.

Jon has come to her door. Several times. She has not mentioned the painting that he took and neither has he. They sit in the middle of the floor and share a glass of wine and he mentions the places he has been with the posters and she nods and fills his glass when it is empty and she waits on him to reach over for her but he hasn't. She wants him to keep coming back. She wants to ask questions about Jennifer, to listen to him talk about her, to know more of the story. She wants him to be vulnerable and sad. With the women it was always the same— she took them for boring, numbed creatures and in her self-proclaimed graciousness she offered them an air of the mysterious. With Jon, she has the living, breathing unknown. She has the questions. The big questions. She believes he will come back and she hopes he will come back unchanged so that the intrigue and the hurt will remain.

She finishes the sandwich, tosses the wrapper and empty Coke into a garbage can next to the gate, and leaves the playground. Walking home, she passes people sitting outside at the cafés, having lunch and coffee and soaking in the warmth. When she comes to Le Café Perdu, she steps inside and looks at the woman she had forgotten about until Jon asked to buy her. She sees what he saw—her waiting, her anxiousness. A waitress approaches Iris and asks if she would like to sit and she says no, takes one more look at the painting, then makes her way for the apartment. She walks quickly, feeling a need to get back to Jennifer.

She enters her building and climbs the stairs, and when she gets to her apartment, the door is pushed open. She steps in and calls out, "Hello?" No answer. She moves through the great room and looks in the kitchen and there is no one. She calls out again and still no answer and she makes her way to Jennifer's room and the door is closed. She reaches to turn the knob and it is locked.

"Hello?" she says and receives no reply. She puts her ear to the door and listens for movement but the room is still. She tries to turn the knob again but it doesn't move. Then she knocks on the door and calls out more forcefully, "Who is in here?"

She waits for a moment, then knocks again and says, "I can call the police."

"Call them," a voice returns.

She touches the door with her fingertips, leans her head against it, and says softly, "You were not supposed to see until I was finished."

Again, quiet follows. Iris sits on the floor, facing the door. She scrapes paint from the palm of her hand with her fingernail. She doesn't know what to say, so she doesn't say anything and waits for Jon to make the next move. Minutes go by and the room on the other side of the door remains as still and quiet as an empty church. Iris crosses her legs and leans back on her elbows. She then stretches her body out in the hallway, her head resting in the palms of folded hands. Finally, she hears footsteps, but they are random, only side to side instead of toward the door. She stares at the ceiling and to pass the time she clicks her tongue on the roof of her mouth.

"Be quiet," Jon says and she stops. Again there are footsteps and Iris sits up and scoots over to the door. She puts her head to the floor and under the doorway she sees Jon's feet close to the door, almost close enough to reach with her fingers. She thinks of wiggling them underneath, but decides he might stomp them. So she stands and holds the doorknob and says, "Do you want to open the door?"

She hears a sigh, then feels the weight of his body fall against the door. "You're a liar," he says.

"I thought you worked during the day," she answers.

"Cut the bullshit, Iris. I swear to God I'm going to rip her into a hundred pieces and throw her out of the window if you don't tell me the truth."

She knows it is a bluff but isn't brave enough to call him on it. "Okay," she says. "I will not bullshit."

"Good."

"Open the door?"

"No. You haven't answered me yet. Why did you lie?"

"Because. Because I changed my mind. I told you it was possible."

"No, you didn't."

"Yes, I did. You didn't listen."

"How many times have you seen me since you started?"

"If you will open the door I can explain better."

"When were you going to tell me?"

"One day."

"That's another lie."

"Jon, it's not a lie. I only needed some time. Now, please. Open the door."

He moves back and bangs his fist on the door and Iris jumps back and lets out a quick scream. "Some time for what?" he yells. "She doesn't belong to you!"

She starts to answer but hears him move away from the door and across the room. "Jon, don't!" she calls out, and then she is interrupted by the easel hitting the floor. She calls out to him again and she knocks on the door. "Jon!"

"I'll do what I want," he answers calmly, and the next sound she expects to hear is that of the canvas ripping.

But instead, the rush of noise is followed by the same stale silence that was there before. As if the room were empty. She presses her cheek to the door. Holds her breath. Waits for what to do next.

"I'm sorry," she says involuntarily, as if it escaped from somewhere other than her mouth. She touches the doorknob again, only to hold it for a moment, then she backs away from the door and walks out of the apartment, closing the apartment door loudly so that he will know she is gone. Out in the street the day feels different than before, the satisfaction of the perfect hours of morning work far away. The smoothness of the sunshine, of her walk, of her smiles that fell on strangers is replaced by an uncomfortable gait with folded arms, by bothersome clouds hovering in the once clear sky. She returns to the playground and the bicycle is gone and a teenage babysitter and a child sit on a bench with a frizzy-haired doll. A café is across the street from the playground and she sits and asks for a small carafe of wine. A thin, young man moves from his table and sits with her and smiles a hopeful smile, but she doesn't smile back and he doesn't sit long. After the second glass of wine is finished, she walks back to the apartment, figuring the painting of Jennifer is gone with Jon. Maybe he will keep her, she thinks. Maybe he will roll her up and carry her around and look at her when he needs to. Maybe I can start again. I know where to find another poster. She comes to her building and climbs the stairs reluctantly, her legs heavy as if tree stumps. She enters the apartment and walks straight to the back room. The door is closed and she wonders if he is still there. She doesn't call out but tries the doorknob and this time it turns, and she pushes the door open and peeks inside. The easel is again standing and Jennifer sits in the same spot she has been sitting all along. She approaches the painting and finds it unscarred. A scrap of paper sits on the easel at the base of the painting and she picks it up. On the paper, Jon has written three questions.

Why did you put her in a classroom?

Why did you show her neck?

Why do you care?

10

In contrast to the earlier months when she found it sinful to move more than several feet from the telephone, Estelle has discovered comfort in motion. Run errands that may or may not need running, wash and fold clothes, go out for the morning and evening editions of the newspaper. Keep moving. She has been tempted to tack the city map up on the kitchen wall and sit with the red markers. Twice she has gone to the hall closet to get the box. And twice she stopped herself at the closet door, wrung her hands, and talked herself into cleaning the bathroom. Jon has told her to stop, that he can't find anything. But he also has told her that the apartment smells like lemons and that he feels better with the windows open. When they sit down to dinner with shiny silverware and a fresh tablecloth, they ignore the fact that there has been no more good news from Marceau.

Throughout all the cleaning, the poster tube and duffel bag have sat in a corner of the bedroom next to a dresser. She has been careful not to touch them. When Estelle sweeps the floors, she avoids the corner. When she puts clean socks and underwear in the dresser, she averts her eyes from the tube and bag as they remind her of the bad. They remind her of the first days of talking to police, of picking out school photographs, of going without sleep for days. The tube stuck under Jon's arm like an appendage, as he never left the apartment without it, while she waited in the apartment, the winter light disappearing early in the evening, closing the apartment walls in on her while she waited and waited and waited. She knows if she picks up the tube and opens it, her next move will be to the kitchen with the map and cigarettes and bar stool. She knows that the duffel bag is empty but that it will have that feel—that feel of the metro halls, of the hands of strangers. Look for the good, she thinks as she avoids the corner as if it were occupied by a pack of rabid dogs.

But today, with fresh towels on the bathroom shelf and the white clothes folded and put away, she sits at the end of the bed and stares at the corner. A dust line changes the shade of the hardwood in front of the bag and tube and forms a dirty triangle as it reaches to the walls. Her hands are on her knees and her right leg bounces nervously. She looks at the clock on the nightstand and she has been sitting and staring for seven minutes, which beats the record of five minutes from two days before. Look for the miracles in the small things, she thinks, but she can't decide if the miracle is in getting up and walking away or conquering the evil in the corner by treating the bag and tube as if they belonged. She stands, claps her hands, and says, "Let's go," then she takes a step toward the door, pauses, and sits back down.

Somebody knock on the door, she thinks. Or call. Ring telephone. Ring. She puts her hands over her face and groans. Falls back on the bed and looks at the ceiling.

Do you have faith? Yes. Then you are healed.

She sits up and looks at the clock. Nine minutes. "This is ridiculous," she says and she goes to the corner and picks up the duffel bag. She shakes off the dust and unzips it. It is empty, as she thought. She tosses it toward the closet, then she reaches for the tube. She unscrews the cap, again expecting to find nothing, but she notices something inside. Something different, the roll of paper thicker than that of the posters and its edges white and frayed. She pinches it and pulls it out of the tube and she unrolls the canvas. It is too large to hold and look at completely, so she lays it on the bed and places books at the four corners. Estelle stands between the open bedroom window and the canvas, so she steps aside to remove her shadow from the faceless woman.

The fresh light seems to awaken the painting. The woman is bare to the waist and her legs are long, her knees turned inward as she sits on concrete steps. She appears to be wearing a slip, the straps fallen off her shoulders, and she leans forward with her elbows on her knees and hands dropping between her legs. Her shoulders are frail, almost pointed. It is uncertain how the slip stays up, covering her chest. Her bare feet are also turned inward. The slip is flesh-toned and slightly lighter than her skin and her hair is brown with faint touches of beige blended throughout. The hair is exceptionally long but falls behind her, careful not to cover her body, its length visible from her sides at the small of the back. The steps are gray like an old coin and the lines of the steps are blurred. The last step is behind the woman's head but the base of the building that begins to appear at the top of the canvas is undistinguished and more blurred than the foreground.

Estelle sits on the bed, leans over the painting, feels the brushstrokes. She looks at the face and touches it and the paint is smoother than on the rest of the canvas. She searches for a signature at each of the four corners, but there isn't one. When she sits close to the painting, looking at it from the side, the woman seems thinner, almost sickly. Estelle touches the woman's hands, the woman's knees. They look fragile, as if they could be broken with a stiff kick. She touches the woman's feet, then she feels the concrete steps, half expecting small bits of gravel to flake off on her fingertips.

She falls back on the bed exasperated, lying parallel to the faceless woman, aware that it can all run together at any moment. Aware that the only thing she can be certain of is that she doesn't know anything. Miracles? The thought of linking them together feels to her now like a weak excuse for optimism. Then she thinks of Jon and is anxious for him to come home. So this is what he does when he's supposed to be putting up the posters and handing out the flyers. She rolls on her side and again looks at the woman and she is unable to decide if he's a son of a bitch or not. His first move when I ask about the painting will tell me. Probably tell me more than I want to know. More than I expect. But if

I expect the worst, she thinks, it won't be so bad. The questions come to her in flashes—how long has the woman been in the tube, where did she come from, is she someone he knows, someone he screws, someone I should hate? The questions keep running until she makes herself stop by looking at the open window and she wonders if falling three flights can kill you, if it would make M. Conrer happy to walk out the front door of the café and be the one who finds her?

Estelle sits up on the edge of the bed, her feet on the floor. It feels like a different day than it had been ten minutes ago. She stares ahead, her eyes wide and blank like an empty tunnel. Then she goes into the hall closet and finds a hammer and a handful of nails. A mirror hangs on the wall over the dresser and she takes it down and leans it in the corner where the tube and bag had been. She removes the books from the corners of the canvas, and hangs the woman on the wall in place of the mirror. Estelle sets the hammer on the dresser, takes a step back, and stares at her curiously.

"Who do you belong to?" she asks.

She kneels and opens the bottom drawer of the dresser. The drawer is where she keeps her lingerie, and as she looks through it she sees colors and touches fabrics she has forgotten. But she knows she has a slip that is flimsy and flesh-colored like the one the woman wears, and after emptying stockings and bras and a boa onto the floor, she finds it pushed toward the back of the drawer.

She stands and undresses, walks naked to the window, and closes the curtains. Then she puts on the slip.

The wall that holds the painting faces the bed and Estelle stacks the three pillows on the bed, then climbs on top and sits, hoping the pillows will mimic the concrete steps. But the pillows sag with her weight and her knees rise too high to prop her elbows on them. She goes into the living room and takes more pillows from the sofa and adds them to the stack. Again, she climbs on top and sits and the stack is higher and firmer. Estelle studies the woman, the way the knees are bent, the angle of the feet. She hikes the slip up around her waist, drops the straps from her shoulders. Dangles her hands between her legs so nothing important shows. Estelle's chest is bigger than the woman's and the slip holds up easier for her, so her arms are more relaxed. The stack of pillows begins to sag with Estelle's movement, so she sets the pose and she pauses, careful not to cause the stack to tip over.

And they look at each other. I should let my hair grow, Estelle thinks. And maybe lose a little weight. And take this paint off my toenails. She relaxes the pose and lets herself go limp. She falls over on the bed, lying on her back. A breeze pushes the curtains and she turns her head and watches the waves of the fabric. Steady, delicate waves. She reaches for a pillow and wraps it with her arms. The air is cool on her legs and she covers them with the bed quilt and puts another pillow under her head. Do you have faith? She doesn't answer herself this time. She closes her eyes and asks again, but before she can decide, she is asleep.

＊

Estelle sleeps away the afternoon as she stays underneath the blanket, the breeze in the window cooler with each passing hour. She woke once and looked at the clock and saw that she had plenty of time before Jon came home and she went back to sleep.

After a restless afternoon at work, Jon makes his way home, the metro ride and the walk filled with the painting of Jennifer. It has been four days since he locked himself in the room with her but he might as well still be there as his thoughts remain trapped. He hasn't been back to see Iris, wanting to give her time to think about what she is doing. At the door of his apartment, he drops his keys, picks them up and drops them again, and screams, *"Merde!"* From across the hall, a shirtless boy peeks his head out of the door, and Jon apologizes. Then he gets the key in the door, goes inside, and finds Estelle asleep, the mirror on the floor, and the woman on the wall. "Great," he says and he drops his keys on the dresser. With the noise, Estelle rolls over, stretches, and sits up, covering herself with the blanket.

"Do you want something to drink?" he asks her. She nods and he goes to the refrigerator and comes back with a beer and a bottle of water. "I think I will drink one of those," she says and points at the beer. Back at the refrigerator, he swaps the water for a beer, then pauses, thinks of what he will say. As if she can hear his thoughts, she calls out, "It is too late."

He returns to the bedroom, hands her the beer, and she pats the bed for him to sit beside her. But he shakes his head and stands.

"Do you want me to ask the questions or do you want to tell me?" she says.

"Maybe you should ask."

This is not what she wants to hear and she pushes away the blanket and stands up. He looks at her and then at the painting, then says, "What the hell are you doing?"

"No. I get to ask the questions. And I want to know what the hell *you* are doing?"

Jon moves his head back and forth between Estelle and the woman in the painting. "I don't understand."

"I don't either."

"What are you doing?" he asks again.

"Stop asking me that. I want to know where this came from and why it was in the tube where the posters were supposed to be. Did you even put them up?"

"Yes, I put them up. Every goddamn one of them. If you went out of the house every now and then, you'd see them."

"I go out of the house."

"Okay. Out of the neighborhood."

"I go out of the neighborhood. Don't make this about me. You are the one who has this," Estelle says and she points at the painting. "Why is she a secret?"

"She's not a secret. I just forgot about her in the tube. That's all."

"Who is she?"

"I don't know who she is. She looks a lot like you right now. Or you look like her. Why are you dressed like that?"

"Where did you get her?"

"I was . . . I was out one day and . . ." he begins to answer, then he trails off. Estelle watches closely and his thoughts scatter behind falling eyes, and it appears certain now that he has done something he wasn't supposed to do.

She sits down on the bed, her back to him. "I don't know why you can't tell the truth," she says, barely above a whisper.

Jon drops his head. A quiet minute passes, then he moves over to the painting. "I don't know what the truth is. We don't have any truths. All we have is question marks and empty hope. I'd give anything for an ounce of truth. A fucking bread crumb of truth."

"We have that. They saw her."

"Weeks ago. They saw her weeks ago and there hasn't been a good phone call since. We don't even know if it was really her."

Estelle turns and faces him and her voice sharpens as she says, "I know it was her. You know it was her. At least you knew when it happened. I could look at you and see that you believed it was Jennifer. Only you have empty hope. I'm trying. You don't try anymore."

"Fine. Only I have empty hope. But it doesn't change anything."

"Yes. It changes everything," Estelle says and she stands from the bed, lets the slip fall off her and to the floor, and she begins to get dressed. When she is done, she drinks from her beer and then says, "If you want to quit, quit. I don't care. And do you want to know something else?"

"Sure, Estelle. Tell me something else."

"I hate you. I hate you and I don't want to see you or that piece of shit in the apartment. Take her and go away from me."

"Just let me explain."

"I don't care, Jon. I don't want you to explain. I don't care what money you wasted to get her or if your girlfriend gave her to you or whatever happened. I don't care why you didn't tell me or why you are such an asshole. Even if you do explain, I don't believe you. You missed the chance. So you leave or I will leave."

Jon takes a step toward her and says, "Estelle—"

"No," she says and she puts her hands up as if stopping traffic.

"Estelle, please."

"Okay. Then I will leave," she says and she moves around him and picks up the duffel bag from the floor. "Move," she says and she pushes him away from the dresser, then she opens the drawers and puts clothes in the bag. Jon watches until the bag is packed and she goes into the bathroom for her toothbrush and shampoo, then he walks into the living room and sits on the sofa and drinks his beer. The bedroom door slams shut behind him.

Estelle takes what she needs from the bathroom, then she walks over to the painting, rips it off the wall, and tosses it on the bed. Then she zips the bag and throws it over her shoulder and walks out of the bedroom. Jon doesn't turn his head when she passes and she leaves the apartment without another word.

The truth, he thinks. Then he gets up for another beer and returns to the same spot. He looks at the pictures on the bookshelf, and the people and their smiles and embraces seem foreign as if they were photographs that came with the frames. He remembers sitting in the same position, with the same beer and the same quiet night after night in Geneva. The pacifying click of the tram passing outside every half hour. The Geneva night air light and clean. Feeling so alone that sometimes it seemed as if he didn't really exist, that he was only a fixture in the world, like a brick house or an umbrella. And I was happy, he thinks. He lights a cigarette and drinks the beer and listens to the traffic passing along the street. He wonders if Estelle is downstairs venting to M. Conrer but he believes she is past that, that her anger is more independent and strong. And if he could see her walking along the street, her steps firm and fast and her shoulders square like a soldier, he would be assured. He finishes the beer and gets up for another, and this time when he sits back down, he notices Estelle's purse on the coffee table, giving him until she returns from trying to check into a hotel to figure out what to say.

He has gone from sitting to lying on the sofa when the apartment door opens and Estelle walks in and looks for the purse.

"Here it is," he says and sits up. He points at the coffee table. She moves around the sofa and picks it up without looking at him. She is only steps from being gone again when Jon says, "Estelle, stop. Please. I'll tell you the truth if you want to hear it."

She stops at the apartment door. "All of it?"

"All of it."

Estelle drops her purse and walks back and sits in the chair.

Jon leans forward, elbows on his knees, sweating a little. "I was out one day putting up our stuff and I stopped in this bar and I saw this painting and I liked it for some reason." He sits back and sighs and says, "I liked it because it made me think about Jennifer. I don't know why. Something about it just made me think about her. The look on her face. It seemed like the way Jennifer might look now. Waiting and wondering. So I went to the artist's studio. It was only a few blocks away. And I met the woman and saw some of her other work and that painting you found is one of them." Jon pauses again, rolls his eyes toward the ceiling.

"And what else?" Estelle asks.

"And so I asked her to paint Jennifer and she said no and I've been going back to try to get her to and she finally started on it and that's that. We can go see it if you want."

Estelle shakes her head. "I thought you said you were going to tell me all of it."

"That *is* all of it, Estelle. It's not that big a deal. I just forgot about the damn thing in the tube."

Estelle stands and walks around the room, behind the couch, looks down at the back of his head. He runs his hand through his hair and says, "Do you want to go or not?"

"Fine," she says, folding her arms. "Let's go."

They walk to the metro and ride to Abbesses. It's a long and quiet ride as if being shared by two people who have never met. When they arrive at the stop, Jon leaves the metro and walks up into the street, Estelle on his heels, following without speaking. During the metro ride, the day has faded and they move in the calm of the twilight. They come to Le Café Perdu and step inside. Jon points to the woman on the wall and says, "That's the first one I saw." Before she can look closer, Jon is out the door and walking toward Iris's apartment. She hesitates, wants to call out to him to wait, let me look, but she doesn't and she hurries to catch up. She keeps a step behind as he turns the corner onto a one-way street. In the middle of the block is Iris's building. Jon goes in and she follows him up the stairs and they stand together at her door.

"Are you sure you want to go in?" he asks.

"Why wouldn't I?"

He shakes his head and bites his lip, then says, "I needed to ask. That's all."

The light in the hallway is out and the small space is filled with shadow. A light shines from beneath Iris's door. Jon knocks and they wait. There is movement, but she doesn't answer, and Jon knocks again and says, "I know you're in there."

"J'arrive," Iris answers. "I am looking for the answers to your questions before I let you in."

"What questions?" Estelle asks.

"Iris. Open the door. I'm not alone."

This time, the door opens, and Iris is as she has always been— old clothes splattered with paint, bare feet, her hair an artistic mess. "Come in," she says.

They all move into the center of the room, the women around them on easels and leaned against walls. Estelle scans the room, then looks at Iris.

"This is my wife," Jon says.

Iris nods and introduces herself and Estelle does the same.

"I hope you don't mind us coming over. Estelle wants to see the painting of Jennifer." When Estelle turns again to the paintings, Jon looks at Iris as if to say quit being stupid and she nods.

"How many are there?" Estelle asks.

"Many. Many have come and gone."

Iris moves over and stands next to Estelle. While they look, Jon slips out of the room and into the bathroom. He closes the door and splashes water on his face, then he sits on the toilet. He hears the women talking and covers his ears. After waiting a few minutes, he gets up and flushes the toilet, then before returning to the big room, he checks the door of Jennifer's room. The knob turns and he pushes the door open and a painting sits on an easel next to the window, but it is covered with a sheet. The scrap of paper with his three questions is on the floor. Iris calls him and he closes the door and rejoins the women and finds them smiling pleasantly as if they were old friends.

"We want to see her," Jon says.

"I'm not finished."

"I don't give a shit. I told you before she's not yours and we want to see her right now. You either show me or I'm taking her."

"Calm down," Estelle says.

"Okay, Jon," Iris says. "We will look. Will you go and get us some wine before?"

"How many times have you been here?" Estelle asks.

"A few. I already told you that, too."

"He likes to watch me work," Iris says.

Estelle looks at Iris in a way that explains to her that she is not a fool.

"I'd like that wine," Jon says.

"No," Estelle answers, looking back at Jon. "I think we should look at the painting. I don't care if it isn't finished."

Iris claps her hands together and rubs them, then says, "She is in the back room. The door is open and a sheet is over her. I think that I will let you look at her together and I will stay here." Iris walks to the window and takes a pack of cigarettes from the ledge. Then she lights one and goes into the kitchen.

"This way," Jon says.

They pass through the hallway and enter the room. Jon turns on the light. Estelle walks over to the easel, stepping over the scrap of paper, and Jon comes behind her and picks it up and stuffs it in his pocket.

"What poster did she use? The new one or the old one?" Estelle asks.

"The new one."

Jon reaches and takes hold of the sheet, but Estelle grabs his arm and says, "Wait."

Jon lets go and says, "What is it?"

"Something," she says. "Something is not right."

"We don't have to look."

But she moves her hand from his arm and nods and this time he takes the sheet with both hands and removes it from the painting. Then he steps back, drops the sheet on the floor, and says, "My God." Estelle covers her open mouth with her hand and she starts to cry.

The classroom setting is gone from the background of the painting and a deep purple surrounds the child, the color reaching every corner of the canvas. Jennifer's neck remains long and bare, her hair remains down, and there is her forehead, eyes, cheeks, and nose, the work stopping just above where the mouth will be. The eyes and cheeks are eager and appear as if, once the face is finished, she will be smiling.

"Jon," Estelle says. He is still as she leans against him. She wipes her eyes and sniffs.

He says quietly, "I didn't expect it to be so much like her."

They stand against each other motionless. Jennifer looks back, so real that if she had a mouth, they would expect words.

"The purple is for faith," Iris says behind them. They turn and look at her. She is wearing shoes and a sweater over her splattered shirt. "I kept putting her in different places but it did not seem right. So I chose a color that I thought might help in some way. When you are finished, lock the door behind you," she says and she leaves.

Estelle sits on the floor and looks up at the child. Jon walks around the room. Outside the window, the twilight has turned to night and a crescent moon is low in the sky. Jon goes into the other room, hoping to find the cigarettes on the windowsill but Iris has taken them. When he returns, Estelle is standing next to Jennifer, and the mother so close to the child reminds him how similar they are.

"I like her hair down," Estelle says.

"It makes her more like you."

"Do you think she's too pale or is it the dark purple?"

"The purple."

"There is much of it. Maybe you will have faith now that Iris has put it here for you."

"Don't say that."

"I will not say things if you will not do things."

He stands against the wall and doesn't answer.

"How many times have you been here?" she asks.

"Estelle. You have asked me that."

"No. I don't mean it like you think I mean it. I don't mean how many times have you walked into this building. You know what I mean."

He looks at his feet, then back to her. "Only once. I swear."

Estelle looks back at the painting and says, "I don't understand you, Jon. Of all the things to quit. You quit Jennifer. You quit me."

"I haven't quit."

"Yes, you have," Estelle says, looking at her daughter's unfinished face. "You have quit or you wouldn't have fucked this woman. Once or twice or twenty times. It doesn't matter. Did you expect me to shrug it off because you say it was only once?"

"I didn't expect anything."

"Exactly."

He moves off the wall, closer to her, and he stops an arm's length away.

"I think you should go," she says.

"Okay. I'll see you at home."

"No. That is not what I mean. I think that you should be the one to leave for a little while. Not me. I will wait here and let you go home and take what you need." She speaks without taking her eyes off the painting. He wants to argue but her indifference has built a wall around her. So he nods, says, "I'll call you later." He touches her shoulder but she is unaffected, and he leaves the apartment.

On the sidewalk in front of Le Café Perdu, he finds Iris smoking. When she notices him, she tosses her cigarette and takes a piece of paper from her pocket. She holds it to him and he asks what it is.

"Don't you want to see my answers to your questions?" she asks.

He shakes his head. "Nope. I don't care what you think. Can't believe I thought I did." He leaves her and goes down into the station, and instead of taking the train home, he takes the train to Solférino and he walks to the bench in front of the Musée d'Orsay and sits. Like the days, the nights are warmer and more welcoming. More people walk along the river. More cameras flash from the Pont des Arts toward the Île de la Cité. More tables make it from the morning to the night along the sidewalks. More taxis are full. In the weeks to come, the crowd will grow, the prices will go up, only the sunshine will be free. An Italian family stops and asks Jon to take their picture and he obliges. He gets a cigarette in return and sits down again. When the cigarette is done, he tosses the butt onto the sidewalk, leans back and stretches out his legs and arms, and says toward the clear night sky, "Where the fuck are you?"

He gets up and walks back to the metro station, needing to hurry home and get out quickly as he has wasted the time Estelle has given him. Going down the stairs, he passes Jennifer's poster and he takes it off the wall, folds it, and puts it in the garbage. Then he opens his wallet to see which credit card he has, and two metro changes later, he is standing at the ticket counter at the Gare de Lyon, buying a ticket for the late train to Geneva.

11

The train leaves the station at 9:34. Jon sits in a smoking car, alone except for a man at the other end who smokes a pipe and blows his nose frequently. He sits next to the window and watches the lights of the houses in the countryside pass by methodically. When the lights disappear and there is only the dark farmland, he reads random sections of random newspapers left behind from the train's daily run. At midnight, the train crosses into Switzerland and stops in Lausanne for forty-five minutes. During the wait, he sits alone in the café car and drinks two beers. He sits facing the station. Passengers trickle off the train and disappear into the station. No one gets on. Finally, the porter blows a whistle and the train departs and arrives in Geneva at two a.m.

As Jon walks, Geneva sleeps, its night lacking the randomness of Paris. Through Centre Ville, the shops and restaurants are closed, the sidewalks clean, the outside tables neatly stacked. He crosses the water and comes to the rue du Rhône. He walks along the trendy, expensive street, mannequins staring back from the windows of boutiques and salons. The lampposts give a dull glow as if rationing the light. The tram has made its last run and the rails won't click again until six a.m. As far as he can see ahead or behind, he is the only one out.

He leaves the shopping district and walks into the Old Town. The cobblestone streets are narrow, the height of the cramped buildings blocking the moonlight. Shutters are closed over shop windows, windows that during the day hold flower boxes and let the light in on fresh bread, decorative chocolate, antiques, cigars. But in the late night the facades are bland and expressionless as if they were hibernating. He twists through the neighborhood, somewhat lost, then found again as he turns a corner and sees the light of the Irish pub shining into the street. He goes to the door and pulls and it is locked. Behind the bar, a young woman with curly blond hair and a tight shirt counts cash. Jon knocks on the door and she looks up and says, "We're closed." He mouths, "I used to work here," and she shrugs her shoulders and begins to count again. He knows of only one other place along the lake that might still be open, but it's a half-hour walk and instead he walks out of the Old Town and to Place Neuve and he sits on the steps of the Musée Rath.

A small concrete island is in the middle of Place Neuve and holds a statue of a man riding a horse, the name and its importance unknown to Jon. Surrounding the streets are the Musée Rath, Le Grand Théâtre, and Le Conservatoire de Musique, the lawns of L'Université de Genève, and the sidewalks that lead into the park of Plainpalais. Five streets cross at the intersection of Place Neuve and give Geneva the look of a hustling, bustling European city during the working hours. On the other side of the intersection from where Jon sits is rue du Conseil-Général, stretching straight like a plastic straw, and without the people on the sidewalk and cars in the street, he can see ahead several blocks to Café Commerce. He reaches for his wallet, takes out a picture of Jennifer in her soccer uniform, and sets it between his feet. From a cathedral somewhere, tenor-toned chimes echo across the city, signaling three a.m.

"Right there," he says to the photograph, and he points. "Right over there, Jennifer. That's where it started. That's where your dad decided it was time for all this to start. Like I was missing something. Like I needed something." He looks toward the café and can see himself moving about the kitchen, pouring a pastis behind the bar, hiring shapely, inexperienced waitresses. Then he imagines himself at the end of a day, upstairs in the apartment with a book or a plate of leftover pasta, with his shoes on the floor and his feet up, the safety of solitude surrounding him like a brick wall. He closes his eyes and wishes tonight were one of those nights. It was a roundabout way to blame himself but it worked. But there would have never been Estelle, he thinks, then he opens his eyes and looks at Jennifer.

A fair trade. And he tries not to imagine who is touching her, the hands of strangers that he feels around his own throat.

He finishes the cigarette and puts away the picture and walks down the steps of the museum. He crosses the intersection and walks along rue du Conseil-Général toward Café Commerce. A tempered excitement fills him, the notion that Lucien is sitting on a bar stool waiting to welcome him home, ready to hand him the keys to the front door and the apartment upstairs. "Thank God," Lucien will say. "You know where everything is. I'm going on holiday." And then after he and Lucien have discussed what to tell his wife if she asks, he will go upstairs and sleep like he hasn't slept in years, a comalike sleep that he will awake from refreshed and eager. He's almost nervous as he gets a block closer and can see familiar tables on a familiar sidewalk, the twelve years that have passed merely a mistake about to be erased.

He crosses the street and stands in front of Café Commerce. Except that it's not Café Commerce. Where CAFÉ COMMERCE had been painted in large letters above the doorway, COMMERCE has been blotted out and replaced with RIVE. CAFÉ RIVE. Jon steps back and looks up and down the street but he is in the right place. Underneath RIVE, the letters of COMMERCE can still be made out underneath a thin coat of paint, and an awkward blank space separates the words CAFÉ and RIVE as RIVE is centered over COMMERCE. He moves a table and cups his hands and looks in the window. The bar has been moved from the right to the left. The tables are fewer and the extra space is filled with two couches. The exposed brick of the back wall of the café has been painted something light, either cream or lavender. Rectangular scraps of mismatched carpet cover the wooden floors underneath the bar stools and tables. And the jukebox that once sat in the corner next to the bathroom door is gone, a video poker machine in its place. The sidewalk tables are all that remain from the place that Jon knew. He steps back from the window, takes a chair off a table, and sits down. He wonders if Lucien is dead.

A Volkswagen turns onto the street and passes Jon, the driver slowing down and staring curiously at the man sitting outside of Café Rive hours early for the day's first coffee. He sits until the cathedral chimes four a.m., then he gets up, takes one more look inside, and he walks away. He takes his time on his way back to the train station, stopping at a park bench along the river, stopping at another park bench in Plainpalais, then having coffee at an early bakery in Centre Ville. The first morning light appears and it is true and welcoming, filtering newness into the cracks and crevices of the sleeping city. Jon leaves the bakery and goes to the train station. He buys a ticket for the earliest train to Paris, then he walks to a row of benches in front of the train station near the taxi stand. He watches the day awake. The tram makes its initial appearance, moving sluggishly as if it would rather be sleeping. Men in suits get out of taxis with their briefcases and check their coat pockets for tickets and passports. Café doors open periodically along the street across from the station, women in house slippers sweeping doorways that don't need sweeping. Dogs on leashes piss on garbage cans and street-sign posts as owners squint and smoke their first cigarette. The morning light changes the sky from gray to a tainted blue. Two security guards join Jon on the bench row and unwrap their breakfast from white paper bags. A recorded female voice sounds throughout the station and outside, announcing departure gates and times. Before the security guards have finished eating, the voice announces Jon's train to Paris. He gets up, stretches, and takes a long look at Geneva.

He turns to the security guards and says in French, "It's like I was never even here." Then he goes to the train, lies across two seats, and falls asleep before the train leaves the station. He doesn't open his eyes again until a porter shakes his shoulder and says, "Monsieur, we have arrived in Paris."

Estelle doesn't sleep all night. She rearranges the kitchen cabinets, watches bits of a movie she has watched bits of before, tries to read but can never make it more than a handful of pages. Everywhere she looks, she sees the painting of Jennifer. And when she is able to rid the image of Jennifer's long neck and bright eyes from her mind, the image of Jon on top of Iris takes its place. She figures she will never sleep again and doesn't care.

At daybreak, she opens the window of the living room and listens to M. Conrer sing as he wipes the dew from the tables and chairs. Then she makes coffee and an omelet and watches the news. After she finishes eating, she goes into the bathroom and runs a bath. She gets undressed and eases into the tub, the water a fraction too hot. She settles and catches her breath and leans her head back on a hand towel. She wonders where Jon has spent the night and is glad it wasn't with her. With her foot she turns the knob for the cold water and brings down the water temperature. Then she shampoos her hair and shaves her legs. She sits until the skin of her fingers and toes begins to wrinkle and she puts on her robe and lies down on the bed. She stares at the empty wall where the mirror, and then the woman, had been. The sound of the day picks up outside, more cars passing, more voices. She lies still for only a moment, then she gets dressed and dries her hair and goes downstairs to the café.

M. Conrer greets her as she comes in. The café is full and he is busy but she pulls him aside and says, "I'm going to help you today. Whatever you need. The only thing I ask is that you do not mention Jennifer to me. Do you promise?"

He waits to answer, reaching out to take her arm, but she turns to avoid being touched. A customer asks for change and M. Conrer nods and says, "I promise."

"Then I'll get the change," she says.

Estelle works like a robot the rest of the morning in the café, not speaking unless it is a necessity. She buses tables, wipes the windows, makes espresso, empties the garbage. She is constant, silent motion, never asking what to do, only doing. As the mornings have warmed, the business has picked up, and M. Conrer has no problem keeping his promise. At 10:30 there is a midmorning lull and she and M. Conrer and the two boys in the kitchen get caught up—the dishes washed, clean glasses stacked behind the bar, the chairs and tables gathered neatly.

"Now we will sit and have our own coffee," M. Conrer says.

Estelle wipes her moist forehead with the sleeve of her shirt, then says, "Thanks, but I have to go. I will come back this afternoon." She kisses him and leaves the café, walking to the newspaper stand on the corner for the morning paper. She looks at the date of the newspaper and doesn't buy it. She walks back to the apartment and she feels refreshed from the sweat as she climbs the stairs, her blood flowing and her mind clear. But that all comes to a halt when she opens the apartment door and Jon is sitting on the sofa.

She closes the door, walks over to him, and says, "What are you doing here?"

"I needed some things." His shoes and coat are off, his shirt untucked. His hair is slick and messy and his eyes are puffy.

"Didn't you come last night?"

"Do I look like it?"

"Just please take what you need and leave," she says, then she goes into the kitchen and pours a glass of juice. He gets up and follows her. She drinks the juice and stares at the spice rack next to the refrigerator. He leans on the counter and watches. She finishes and sets the glass in the sink and says, "You smell."

"Do you mind if I take a shower?"

"Yes," she says and she moves past him. She takes a cigarette from her purse and stands next to the open window of the living room. Again, he follows, as if walking in her footsteps will gain him grace.

"Do you understand?" she turns and says. "Which language do you prefer? English or French?"

"Estelle," he says, then he pauses, folds his arms, and sways from side to side.

She smokes and ignores him.

"Estelle," he says again.

She turns to him, irritated, and says, "What?"

He looks past her, out of the window. "Nothing," he says and he goes into the bedroom to pack.

She finishes the cigarette and lights another as she waits on him to leave. He comes back with a suitcase and sits on the couch and puts on his shoes. Then he takes his coat from the back of the couch and lays it across his lap.

"The past doesn't matter at all," he says. "It's getting harder to remember when life was any different than it is right now. I was thinking last night that if only I would have made a turn here or there, that we wouldn't be here. You'd be off with some handsome man, living down south. A couple of kids. We might've passed on the street one day and never even glanced at one another. Or not even that. I'd probably never have made it to Paris. Only a slight turn, nothing special. If I would've taken the late train that day from Geneva. Or even if it was the same train, the lady at the desk could have given me seat twelve instead of twenty-two or whatever it was. But then I decided that none of that matters. Somehow, we'd still be sitting right here, looking at one another. Jennifer would still be gone. You'd still want me out. M. Conrer would still have that stupid smile on his face every time he tells me everything is going to be all right. I don't know what the point is in decisions. You said something one time about the finger of God on your head, how it felt protective. I believe it's there but not like that. More like He's pushing and pulling us like puppets. Like mindless, wooden puppets who don't get a say in what goes on down here. The Great Puppeteer is how I'll start the next time I decide to ask for Jennifer back. If there is a next time."

Estelle tosses her cigarette out of the window and sighs.

"What do you think?" he asks.

She leans on the window ledge and looks around the apartment, then to him. "I think you are lost. More lost every day."

He nods. "Are you?"

"No. I know where I am. It doesn't matter why. If He's pushing and pulling us, then so be it. I don't have time to think about it."

"That's all we have is time. Handfuls of it. We have so goddamn much I don't know what to do with it," Jon says, then he gets up and takes the suitcase. He walks to the apartment door and sets it down, then he comes back into the living room and says, "I didn't get to ask you what you thought of the painting."

"Once she is finished, I'd like to have her. Do you think that she will give her to us?"

"I think so."

"Are you going to stay with her?"

"No, Estelle. It's nothing like that. I tried to tell you."

"I don't want to know any more about it. This is probably what you think we do. This is France, right? We all sleep with each other and smile into the same mirror every day, like changing women is the same as changing socks."

"Don't lecture me. I'm not new to this and I'm sure as hell not some naive American living out his fantasies."

"Then act like it."

He wants to move to her and kiss her but knows he can't. "I'll call and let you know where I am," he says, then he picks up his wallet and keys from the kitchen counter and he leaves the apartment. Estelle leans out the window and watches him walk out of the building and into M. Conrer's café, leaving the suitcase on the sidewalk.

"He'll be drunk in half an hour," she says, then thinks it isn't such a bad idea and she opens a bottle of wine and sits on the floor of the living room. She turns on the television and spreads the newspaper out in front of her. She looks for and finds the classified section and the telephone rings.

She shakes her head, believing it is either Jon or M. Conrer. She opens the classifieds to the pets and looks for a puppy. The phone continues to ring. "Son of a bitch," she says and she crawls over to the wall to unplug it and the machine answers. She stops to listen when she hears Marceau.

"Estelle and Jon, this is Detective Marceau. If you are there, pick up the telephone."

Estelle knocks the receiver to the floor, fumbles it, then picks it up and says, "Yes?"

"Estelle? Is Jon with you?"

"Yes. I mean, sort of. He's downstairs. What is it?"

"Two days ago at the train station in Brussels, a five-year-old boy who was being abducted from the bathroom broke away and ran screaming through the station. The police arrested a man, who led us to another man. We traced him to a house on the outskirts of Lille. We need you and Jon to come to the police station and I will explain the rest."

"No. Don't do that to me. Explain the rest."

"I think it's better if you are together."

"We are together. He's downstairs. Tell me now."

Someone speaks to Marceau in the background and he covers the phone and answers. Estelle hears only mumbles and she screams, "Marceau! Tell me now!" She rises from her knees and waits, the mumbling like the beating of drums off in the distance. She breathes hard as she waits, then again she screams into the telephone, but the mumbling continues.

Marceau returns and apologizes, her screams seemingly unheard, and he says calmly, "It is very simple, Estelle. I need you and Jon to come to the station because we have Jennifer."

12

She drops the phone and runs to the window and yells, "Jon! Jon!" Then she rushes out the apartment and down the stairs and he is coming out of the door of the café.

Her thoughts are quicker than her mouth and it is difficult to get out, but she manages, "Marceau, Jon. Jennifer, Jennifer. They have Jennifer." Then she turns and runs for the metro and Jon chases after her. Too many people crowd the sidewalk, the train is too slow, the streetlights won't change when they want them to. They make it to the police station much quicker than it seems and they push through a crowd gathered on the front steps. The bottom floor of the police station is divided by a wide, marble hallway and Marceau's office door is at the other end. They weave through janitors and uniformed police holding folders and go into a large room with a high ceiling shared by the detectives and their secretaries. Marceau's desk is in the back in front of a window and they hurry through the maze of cubicles and he is sitting on his desk waiting for them. He is without the overcoat and his sleeves are rolled up and he grins with his mouth closed.

"Where is she?" Estelle asks. She and Jon are breathing fast, their faces flustered.

Marceau reaches to greet them with his hands but neither reaches for him and Jon says, "Where is she?"

"She is okay. Please, just a moment."

"Marceau," Estelle says.

"I am not keeping you because I want to but I have to speak with you a moment. Please. Sit down. This will take two minutes. The sooner we talk, the sooner we see her." He motions them to sit in the wooden chairs they stand next to and he stands between them.

"Now," he says. "I want you to understand that she doesn't look the same right now. Her hair has been shaved and she has lost weight. A doctor has looked at her and she is going to be fine but she is different. Take a breath and understand this. It is important that you don't let her appearance shock you."

Estelle and Jon look at each other, then back at Marceau. "We understand," Jon says. "Is that it?"

Marceau walks around and stands behind the desk. "There is one other thing and this may change when she sees you, but she hasn't spoken since we found her. She was in a closet, gagged and blindfolded, and I get the idea that she wasn't allowed to speak but I don't know for sure. But she hasn't said a word. Like I said, we hope this will change when she sees her parents."

Estelle stands and says, "I don't want to hear any more of this." Then Jon stands and says, "Me either. I understand what you're trying to do but take us to her." Marceau nods and says, "Follow me."

They follow Marceau out into the hallway and up a flight of stairs. After the stairs, he goes into a door that leads down a thin hallway. He stops at the second door on the left. "She is in here with a nurse," he says and he opens the door. Marceau motions for the nurse to leave the room and Jon and Estelle go in. The child sits on a cot with a blanket draped around her shoulders. Jennifer sees them and she says, "I tried," then she begins to cry and they race to touch her.

13

It is late in the summer and the afternoon is humid and clear. A couple and an infant sit on a blanket with a picnic lunch. The infant is a new crawler and moves anxiously from side to side on the blanket, the parents barricading the child from crawling off the blanket and into the grass. The couple is young, blond stubble on the man's face and the woman's hair highlighted an array of browns and reds. The woman is barefoot and the man wears a white T-shirt and his arms are lean and tanned. Occasionally, the man will lift the child and toss him, or her, into the air and the child grins and claps closed fists together. Then the man will set the infant back down and the child crawls until it bumps into its mother's legs and then it turns around and heads back across the length of the blanket.

Jon lies on his side on his own blanket and watches the couple and infant. Estelle and Jennifer try to get a kite into the air, running freely across the open space of the park. Jon has already tried and failed with the kite but Jennifer seemed interested in the effort and so now Estelle works with her, hoping to catch the perfect breeze that will lift the rainbow-striped kite into the air. The couple and infant are in Jon's line of vision of Estelle and Jennifer, and when there is a delay in their effort, a tangled string or dead air, Jon watches the new family as if he knows them.

The summer has set records for both heat and lack of rain. A free production of *Romeo and Juliet* scheduled for the garden of the Musée

Rodin was canceled because the actors feared collapse wearing the heavy Elizabethan costumes. A hardware store in Jon and Estelle's neighborhood gave away rain gauges as a promotion, hoping to conjure up storm clouds. The river sits low and the city has cut back on the hours that the public fountains run. But the summer is almost over and the temperatures are beginning to creep down. Half of Paris is hopeful for a rainy autumn and the other half is bitter that they have to hope for a rainy autumn that will clump the fallen leaves and cause the winter to hurry on. The only ones that haven't noticed the dry gardens and park lawns are the ones who get on planes after they check out of their hotels and go home.

Jennifer yells, "Look!" and Jon sees the kite rise into the air and maintain as Estelle runs with the kite string. The couple with the infant also turns and looks and Jennifer stands with her arm raised and finger pointed skyward. Others across the lawn who have heard Jennifer's cry look up and smile and tell their children to look at the kite. Jon sits up. Jennifer puts her hand over her eyes to shield the sun. The moment lasts for as long as Estelle can keep running, which isn't long, and when she's done and the kite swirls to the ground, heads turn back to cool drinks or conversation. Estelle bends over, winded, her hands on her knees. Jennifer looks at Jon and he waves but she doesn't wave back and she goes to Estelle and helps her gather the kite and string. They walk past the couple and infant, who are picking up to leave, and sit down with Jon. Estelle still hasn't caught her breath and Jon says, "You need some work."

"At least we got it in the air, didn't we?" Estelle answers and looks at Jennifer.

Jennifer nods and takes a bottle of water from a plastic bag they brought with them that is filled with drinks and sandwiches and chips. "I want to run with it next time," she says.

The suggestion pleases her parents and then Estelle says, "We'll try again in a few minutes. Do you want to eat something?" Again Jennifer nods and she takes a tuna sandwich from the bag.

"I think I saw an ice cream cart on the other side of the park. Would you like some?" Jon asks.

"Later," Jennifer says.

Again, her response pleases them because these answers are more of the answers of their Jennifer. The Jennifer who was athletic and energetic and never turned down a dessert. The Jennifer who sits in front of them now shows glimpses of that child through the quiet stares and one-word sentences and each glimpse is met with wide smiles.

It will be a work in progress. Be patient. You are one of the lucky ones. These phrases, and others like them, have been given to Jon and Estelle over and over by the voices of children's services. The words float in their minds when they look at Jennifer. Whether it is a doctor, or a therapist, or a social worker, the clichés sit on the tips of their tongues, as common as hello or good-bye. The first time that the therapist said to them that they were lucky, Jon said, "You have a strange idea of luck."

"In your case, life itself is luck," he answered. He was a sleek, smart-looking man with a pointed chin and Jon didn't like him from the start.

"I don't believe in luck," Estelle said.

"Me either," Jon said.

"Whatever you believe in, you may attribute her return to that. Not many children return after they have been missing for more than two days, let alone months."

"We know," Jon said and the next day he complained to children's services that he didn't want a therapist assigned to his daughter who would tell them each week how fucking lucky they were. Estelle stood next to him in the kitchen as he spoke on the telephone, nodding and holding his arm. After he hung up the phone, he asked her if she knew she was touching him.

"Yes," she said.

"I hoped so. You can whenever you want."

"Sometimes I want to," she said. "But sometimes I don't want anything."

"Maybe just a little now and then. Like this. Just touch my arm or hand. Small things."

"You sound like the people we talk to about Jennifer. Everything has to be so small now. I feel like an inchworm."

He had apologized to Estelle in letters, in cards, in phone calls from work. The urge to do it again rose in him and she saw it coming and stopped him.

"Maybe," she said.

"Maybe what?" he asked.

"Only maybe."

Jennifer finishes her sandwich and says, "I'm ready."

"Why don't you try by yourself?" Estelle asks. "And then I'll come along if you need me."

She ponders it a moment, looks across the park at other children playing alone, no adult in sight. She picks at the grass and says, "Promise you'll watch?"

"We're right here, we promise," Jon says.

Jennifer takes the kite and walks into a clear stretch of grass, plenty of room to run. She turns and says, "Watch."

"Go ahead. It's okay," Estelle says. Then she whispers to Jon, "I hate this."

"They said to help her try things again on her own. She's right there. She can do it." He reaches over and holds her hand and she lets him.

Even on the best of days, it has been difficult to shake the image of Jennifer sitting on the cot in the small room at the police station. Fifteen pounds were missing from her already thin frame. Her head was shaved and her lips badly cracked from dehydration. She wore a hospital gown and her dirty, soiled clothes were piled on the floor. Her wrists had rope burns from being bound so tightly. It took them two weeks to gather the nerve to ask Marceau what they found out from the man they arrested.

"There is something very troubling occurring between here and Brussels," he said. He sat with them in their living room on a chair brought from the kitchen table, his legs crossed and his hat in his lap.

Estelle and Jon sat on the edge of the couch, uncomfortable but ready for some answers. "It is almost like a game. Children are disappearing and becoming a sort of currency. As far as we can tell, there is a system in place where these children can be exchanged for one another. No money is involved. The people meet, size up what the other has, and will trade the children as if they were used cars. We believe that this is what happened to Jennifer the day the woman reported seeing her, that the men with her had either just traded for her or were on their way to swap her for another child. The man that we found Jennifer with was the third person to have her. You can imagine how difficult this is making things for us with these children constantly on the move from city to city, or in some cases from country to country." Marceau spoke without emotion, describing the situation as if he were describing a bowl of soup.

"Then why was she in such bad shape?" Jon asked.

"That's the same question we asked and the man told us that this is the way she was given to him. He had planned to clean her up but hadn't gotten around to it. Otherwise, we'll have to wait until she is ready to talk to fill in the blanks."

And they continue to wait, but after four months, she hasn't been ready to talk about the time from her abduction until the time of her return. Not to the police, not to the therapist, not to Estelle and Jon. They know what the medical reports told them but they only waited on Jennifer. Estelle and Jon have not allowed anyone to push her, believing that Jennifer will talk when she's ready, though they would prefer all the answers, no matter how harsh, to what their imagination has done with the missing time. The only thing that Jennifer has disclosed is how it happened. How she was bored at the museum, and while the class was moving from one painting to another, she skipped out and went to the restaurant on the top floor. After a candy bar and Coke, she went to return to the group but they had moved into another area of the museum and a short, balding man in a navy-blue suit asked her if she was lost. When she said yes, he explained that he worked for the museum and that he thought her group had gone outside to the school bus. He put his hand on her shoulder and walked her out of the front doors of the museum, then around to the side and to the back. The bus was there and they walked to it but it was empty, and on the other side of the bus was a van. A man in a similar suit got out and approached them and they forced her into the van. Jennifer gave this account a week after returning home, sitting at the police station at Marceau's desk, a tape recorder running and her parents flanking her. She stopped twice to say that she tried to get away, tried to scream, tried to fight, as if she needed to prove that it wasn't her choice.

Estelle takes a bag of potato chips from the plastic bag. She offers one to Jon and he declines. Then she says, "She's looking better."

"Still too thin," Jon says.

"I know. But her hair, her face. She's getting there, right?"

They watch Jennifer, and if they didn't know her, she could easily be taken for a boy. Her hair has grown slowly and is darker than before and her knees and elbows appear to have their own agenda as her thin frame runs with the kite string. She stumbles and falls as she looks back to see if the kite is in the air. Jon starts to get up, but Jennifer gives an "I'm okay" wave.

"Is she sleeping any better?" Jon asks. Estelle and Jennifer moved into the big bed when she came home, leaving Jon on the couch. Most nights are filled with shouts from dreams, panic in the dark. There has been no mention of Jennifer moving back into her own room.

"Not really," Estelle says.

School begins in a week but Jennifer will not go. She doesn't want to see friends, ashamed of her appearance. "Not until my hair comes back," she says and her parents agree. And there have recently been more complex questions from her. "Does everyone know?" she asked Estelle in the grocery store. Then later in the day, as the three of them ate lunch at M. Conrer's café, she asked, staring between them, "What do I tell people?"

"We'll talk about that later," Jon said after exchanging an empty look with Estelle, but neither has figured out how to answer. The therapist warned them to be prepared for such questions, but it was like being told to prepare for a bullet.

Jennifer calls for her mother to come and help and Estelle hands Jon the bag of chips and goes to her. Jon mindlessly finishes the chips though he's not hungry. He wonders if Iris found the note he slid under her door earlier in the week. *Have you finished?* is all it said. It was the first time he had been back to see her since Jennifer's return. He figures Iris knows, as it was on the news and in the newspaper, and he wonders if the popularity of Jennifer's return may have dissuaded the portrait's completion, the subject now too mainstream for Iris. Estelle mentioned the painting of Jennifer as they sat up one night and listened for Jennifer to call out in her sleep, and Jon was happy to answer honestly that he hadn't been back.

"Do you still want it?" she asked.

"No," he said. "Do you?"

"No. Not really."

But he took her interest as a kind of permission, and the next afternoon after work, he stopped at Iris's apartment. The door was locked. No sound from inside. He scribbled the note and slid it under the door and left relieved.

Estelle and Jennifer have little luck without a breeze and they return to the blanket. "Would you like the ice cream now?" Jon asks.

"Okay," Jennifer says. "Vanilla on the inside, chocolate on the outside."

"Me too," Estelle says and Jon promises to be right back.

He follows a curvy pebble pathway across the park, avoiding bicycles and soccer balls as he walks with his hands in his pockets. He looks over his shoulder now and then at Jennifer and Estelle. He comes to the ice cream cart and stands in line behind a teenage couple holding hands, twin girls no older than Jennifer, and an old man who wears a sweater despite the heat. As he waits he looks across the park. The sun has fallen in the afternoon sky and many find relief in the growing shadows of the trees. The breeze picks up and he hopes to make another attempt with the kite, to show Jennifer that it can be done. He moves up in line and buys what Jennifer and Estelle asked for, and walking back, he feels the ice cream already beginning to melt, so he begins to trot. Back at the blanket, his wife and daughter lie on their backs, hands behind their heads.

"Better eat it fast," he says and they sit up and Jennifer thanks him.

"No napkins?" Estelle asks and he shakes his head.

Halfway through the ice cream, the drips have made their hands sticky and Jon holds the plastic bag while they toss away what's left. Jennifer says, "Can we go?"

"Sure," Estelle answers. "There's a fountain by the gate and we can wash our hands." The three of them stand and Jon folds the blanket and puts it over his shoulder. Estelle picks up the plastic bag. Jennifer stands between her mother and father and takes a hand from each of them. They walk at a leisurely pace across the park, the sun behind them and their shadow before them, their silhouette providing a glimpse of what they used to be as they make their way home.

ACKNOWLEDGMENTS

I would like to thank M. Scott Douglass for his early support of this Parisian story, Douglas Mackaman for the time provided at the Abbey in Pontlevoy, France, and Robin Miura and Ellen Levine for keeping this novella alive and well. And as always, I want to thank the three girls that are with me each day.

CPSIA information can be obtained
at www.ICGtesting.com
Printed in the USA
JSHW020257181122
33401JS00002B/7